The New York

PUBLIC PROFILES

Civil Rights Advocates

EDUCATIONAL PUBLISHING
BOOKS

THE NEW YORK TIMES EDITORIAL STAFF

Published in 2020 by New York Times Educational Publishing
in association with The Rosen Publishing Group, Inc.
29 East 21st Street, New York, NY 10010

First Edition

The New York Times
Alex Ward: Editorial Director, Book Development
Phyllis Collazo: Photo Rights/Permissions Editor
Heidi Giovine: Administrative Manager

Rosen Publishing
Megan Kellerman: Managing Editor
Wendy Wong: Editor
Greg Tucker: Creative Director
Brian Garvey: Art Director

AUG 1 4 2020

Cataloging-in-Publication Data
Names: New York Times Company.
Title: Civil rights advocates / edited by the New York Times editorial staff.
Description: New York : New York Times Educational Publishing,
2020. | Series: Public profiles | Includes glossary and index.
Identifiers: ISBN 9781642822397 (library bound) | ISBN
9781642822380 (pbk.) | ISBN 9781642822403 (ebook)
Subjects: LCSH: African Americans—Civil rights—Southern
States—History—20th century—Juvenile literature. | African
American—Civil rights workers—Juvenile literature. | Civil rights
workers—United States—Juvenile literature. | Civil rights
movements—United States—20th century—Juvenile literature.
Classification: LCC E185.96 C585 2020 |
DDC 323.1196'0730904—dc23

Manufactured in the United States of America

On the cover: Civil rights demonstrators walk with placards at
the March on Washington, August 28, 1963; Bob Parent/Hulton
Archive/Getty Images.

Contents

CHAPTER 2

Freedom Riders

CHAPTER 3

Martin Luther King Jr. and Coretta Scott King

CHAPTER 4

Malcolm X

Introduction

IN THE 1950S, black Americans, burdened by the systemic oppression and inferior treatment they encountered, organized and protested to end racial discrimination. They worked to overthrow the Jim Crow laws that upheld racial segregation throughout the South and establish equal rights in the United States. This period of time, spanning over a decade, came to be known as the civil rights movement.

In a time where protests and social movements were almost unheard of, African-Americans' actions, carried out through various demonstrations such as public speeches, sit-ins and marches, forever changed the way people of color were treated and able to live in the United States. Men, women and children came together and protested for simple liberties such as riding a bus, eating lunch at a restaurant or going to school. They sought social and legal action, highlighting the injustices they had faced and reaching out to law enforcement and American citizens to join them in correcting a wrong that had gone unchecked for decades. They persisted despite all the threats and violence they encountered. They wanted black voices to be heard and black bodies to be respected. They wanted to be recognized as humans and as equals.

These calls to action were not organized and carried out on two or three people's shoulders alone. It took hundreds of ordinary citizens to do extraordinary things, and all of their contributions were crucial in taking steps forward for equality. Rosa Parks refused to give up her seat on the bus. Thurgood Marshall's tremendous work as a lawyer for the N.A.A.C.P., which itself was an organization at the forefront of fighting for black rights, compelled the Supreme Court to strike down segregation in schools and allowed progress to take root in the legal

American civil rights campaigner Rev. Dr. Martin Luther King Jr. and his wife Coretta Scott King lead a black voting rights march from Selma, Ala., to the state capital in Montgomery in March 1965.

system. A. Philip Randolph and Bayard Rustin organized the March on Washington. Four black students bravely sat and asked for service at a Woolworth whites-only lunch counter, one of the most well-known sit-ins of the movement. The SCLC, CORE and SNCC all made irreplaceable contributions to the cause, planning rallies and meeting with political figures to give advice on legislation.

However, among these figures were those who also became emblems of social action in the media. These leaders inspired and swept the nation into a frenzy with their perseverance in the face of doubt and hatred. Their actions and words gained nationwide attention and had a country clinging to every piece of news. The Little Rock Nine were students aspiring to receive a better education to put them on equal footing with their peers. Daisy Bates, their mentor and head of the Arkansas branch of the N.A.A.C.P., protected their best interests and guided them toward successful school integration. The Freedom Riders were a diverse collective that set out to test existing laws in public transportation segregation. Others, such as Martin Luther King Jr., Coretta Scott King and Malcolm X, had very different approaches. Yet all three took to the front lines with a long history of advocating for equality and encouraging their fellow black citizens to mobilize and have pride in their identity.

Though these public figures encountered much scrutiny and doubt throughout their lives, their impact on society lives on. They shined a spotlight on lawmakers' ineptitude and struggled for African-Americans to receive the protection and equality they deserved as citizens. They made sure an entire community could no longer be silenced and forced into compliance. These landmark actions have been immortalized in history as some of the most crucial stepping stones of the civil rights movement.

CHAPTER 1

Daisy Bates and the Little Rock Nine

On May 17, 1954, the Brown v. Board of Education case struck down segregation in schools. A few years later, nine black boys and girls enrolled in Central High School in Little Rock, Ark. This became a high-profile case documenting the ongoing tension in Little Rock as they were met with angry mobs, threats from other students and an uncooperative governor. Despite this, they remained determined and were able to attend classes thanks to encouragement and guidance from Daisy Bates, president of the Arkansas branch of the National Association for the Advancement of Colored People (N.A.A.C.P.).

Militia Sent to Little Rock; School Integration Put Off

BY BENJAMIN FINE | SEPT. 3, 1957

LITTLE ROCK, ARK., TUESDAY, SEPT. 3 — Gov. Orval E. Faubus sent militiamen and state police last night to Little Rock High School, where racial integration had been scheduled to start today.

The Governor, a foe of integration, said troops were necessary to prevent violence and bloodshed at the school.

By early morning about 100 members of the state militia had surrounded the school. They were armed with billy clubs, rifles and bayonets. Some carried gas masks.

The Board of Education met with Dr. Virgil Blossom, Superintendent of Schools, late last evening to consider the new developments. It then issued a statement appealing to Negroes not to attempt to pass through the line of troops. The board's statement said:

"Although the Federal Court has ordered integration to proceed, Governor Faubus has said schools should continue as they have in the past and has stationed troops at Central High School to maintain order.

"In view of the situation, we ask that no Negro students attempt to attend Central or any other white high school until this dilemma is legally resolved."

The Federal District Court last Friday upheld a previous court order that integration should begin today. Judge Ronald N. Davies, in a special hearing Friday afternoon, enjoined any and all persons from interfering with the integration program. Judge Davies acted after a county judge, Murray O. Reed, had issued an injunction against integration.

School officials did not know what the next legal move would be.

Twelve Negroes had been scheduled to attend the high school this morning.

The militia at the school is under the direction of Maj. Gen. Sherman T. Clinger. General Clinger would not say whether he would keep out any Negro students who might attempt to enter.

"We will do everything necessary," he said, "to preserve the peace. That is our mission as given to us by the Governor."

In his television talk last night, Governor Faubus said he was calling out the militia because he had heard that violence would break out when schools opened.

He said that many persons in Little Rock had purchased knives and other weapons. He also said that a number of revolvers had been taken from high school students, both white and Negro.

"I have reports of caravans that will converge upon Little Rock from many parts of the state and members of the caravans are to assemble peaceably upon the school grounds in the morning. Some of these groups have already reached the city."

The Governor also said that there was a telephone campaign going on in the city calling on the mothers of white children to assemble on the school grounds at 6 o'clock this morning.

Because of these threats of disorder, violence and possible bloodshed, he said, he has called out the National Guard. However, he said that even with the Guardsmen present, keeping the peace might be difficult.

"I must state here in all sincerity, that it is my opinion, yes, even a conviction, that it will not be possible to restore or to maintain order and protect the lives and property of the citizens if forceable integration is carried out tomorrow in the schools of this community," the Governor said.

"The inevitable conclusion, therefore, must be that the schools in Pulaski County, for the time being, must be operated on the same basis as they have been operated in the past."

"This is a decision," Governor Faubus said, "that I have reached prayerfully, after conferences with dozens of people. The mission of the state militia is to maintain order. They will not act as segregationists or integrationists but as soldiers."

ASKS FOR PUBLIC PEACE

He said that even with the militia it might not be possible to maintain order if "forceful integration is carried out tomorrow."

Governor Faubus said:

"The inevitable conclusion is that the schools must be operated as they have in the past. I appeal to the reason of all. Let us all be good citizens. The public peace will be preserved."

"This is a situation not of my making," he said. "The plan for integration has been set up by the Little Rock school board and the superintendent. The majority of the people of this community are opposed to integration."

Under the plan integration will take place on a gradual basis. This fall the senior high schools will have mixed classes. In 1960, if all goes smoothly, Negroes will be admitted to the junior high school. By 1963 the elementary grades will be thrown open to all students, regardless of color.

Thus, in six years, under the plan, the entire school system will be integrated.

Extremists on both sides are unhappy.

The National Association for the Advancement of Colored People has declared six years to be too long a period. It brought a Federal suit to hasten integration, but the judges ruled that the School Board had shown good faith and was proceeding with all deliberate speed.

The White Citizens Councils and other anti-integrationist groups oppose any degree of integration now or at any foreseeable time.

Amis Guthridge, attorney for the Capital Citizens Council, a local of the Arkansas White Citizens Councils, said today that "we will continue to fight in a peaceful manner to maintain the high principles upon which our Southern society was founded."

It was at seemingly the eleventh hour that Governor Faubus jumped into the fight to prevent integration. He appeared last week at a State Chancery Court hearing on an injunction petition brought in the name of the League of Central High Mothers.

He told the court that there would be rioting and bloodshed if the city program was put into effect and that the Federal Government would not intervene. He urged that the school board be enjoined from going ahead with its plans. An injunction was granted by Chancellor Murray O. Reed of the court.

Granting of the injunction was immediately challenged by the school officials. They cited that they were under orders from the Federal District Court to integrate without delay. The issue was resolved Friday afternoon when Federal Judge Ronald N. Davies overruled the state decision.

In its planning the board of education has taken into consideration the possibility of violence, Dr. Blossom has met with police officials and with other community leaders on steps to avoid conflict.

Arkansas Troops Ban Negro Pupils; Governor Defiant

BY BENJAMIN FINE | SEPT. 5, 1957

LITTLE ROCK, ARK., SEPT. 4 — The state militia barred nine Negro students from the white high school here today.

Fully armed, the troops kept the Negroes from the school grounds while an angry crowd of 400 white men and women jeered, booed and shouted, "go home, niggers." Several hundred militiamen, with guns slung over their shoulders, carrying gas masks and billy clubs, surrounded the school.

The nine Negro students said that they would again attempt to enter the all-white Central High school tomorrow morning.

The troops acted under direct orders of Gov. Orval E. Faubus. In a news conference in his office, Governor Faubus said he would not permit Negroes to enter white schools in this city, despite the order from the Federal District Court. He insisted that he was not flouting the court's orders, but acting to preserve peace and to prevent bloodshed.

'UNWARRANTED INTERFERENCE'

Late tonight Governor Faubus sent a telegram to President Eisenhower asking him to stop the "unwarranted interference of Federal agents in this area."

The Governor declared that he would not cooperate with the Federal agents now investigating his use of troops to block integration here.

The Governor also said in his telegram that he had reason to believe that the telephone lines to his executive mansion "have been tapped." He suspected that the Federal agents were tapping his wires.

"The situation in Little Rock and Arkansas grows more explosive by the hour," the Governor wired.

Meanwhile, Mayor Woodrow W. Mann of Little Rock, the capital of Arkansas, denounced Governor Faubus for having sent the militia into the city.

SEES TENSION CREATED

He said he deeply resented "the wholly unwarranted interference with the internal affairs of this city by the Governor."

The Mayor declared that the Governor had called out the National Guard to "put down trouble where none existed."

"He did so," the Mayor said, "without request from those of us who are directly responsible for the preservation of peace and order. The only effect of his action is to create tensions where none existed.

"If any racial trouble does develop the blame rests squarely on the doorstep of the Governor's mansion," he added.

The open defiance of a Federal Court order by the Governor is the first time that the issue of Federal versus state authority has been reached on the integration problem.

This action set the stage for the first major test of the United States Supreme Court's decision of May, 1954, that racial segregation in schools is unconstitutional.

Federal Judge Ronald N. Davies acted as soon as he learned that his order to integrate the school had been flouted. He asked the Assistant United States Attorney, Osro Cobb, to study the case. He also met with R. Beal Kidd, United States marshal, to discuss the situation.

The Judge asked Mr. Cobb to make an immediate study.

"You are requested to begin at once a full, thorough and complete investigation," Judge Davies said, "to determine the responsibility for interference with the integration order, or responsibility for failure to comply with the order of the court, and to report your findings to me "with the least practicable delay."

Schools opened here yesterday. The school board, when informed that troops would surround the school, had asked the Negro students not to enter. They did not attempt to enter. However, when Judge Davies last night ordered the board to integrate the school the students were told they could come this morning.

The day began quietly. At 6 A. M. only a handful of men and women had gathered in front of the school. About 100 troops were on duty. Many sat at the edge of the sidewalk; some sprawled on the hard cement, their rifles lying beside them.

"It looks kinda quiet," a guardsman said.

"I sure hope it stays that way," another said.

"Just think," one of them said, "we're making history."

"Not me," his khaki-clad companion retorted. "I'd rather go fishing than make history in this hot sun."

Slowly the crowd gathered. By 8 o'clock about 100 men and women were standing quietly across the street from the school. They seemed to be in a jovial mood.

"We sure kept the niggers out," one said. "They won't dare show their faces here."

Slowly the crowd grew until 400 were standing in front of the school. The sun now shone brightly. It would be another hot day.

'HERE THEY COME'

Suddenly a cry came from one end of the street. "A nigger, they're coming, here they come."

A frightened 15-year-old Negro girl, Elizabeth Eckford had sought admission to the school. The troops barred her way and now she had to go through the blocked-off street to the other exit, some 100 yards.

As the girl walked slowly toward the exit, the crowd surrounded her, jeered and yelled. From time to time several troops used their clubs to push the crowd back to prevent anyone from molesting her.

"Don't let her in, go back where you came from," the crowd yelled.

A 15-year-old high school student tried to reach the frightened girl. The troops prevented the Negro girl from being harmed.

A 15-year-old Negro boy, Terrence Roberts, advanced to the school ground. This time the guards formed a human fence and did not let him pass.

"Keep away from our school, you burr head," someone shouted.

The boy had a shiney new yellow pencil over his left ear and he wore an open sports shirt.

He told the guards:

"I was told if there is any resistance and if I'm not permitted to go in not to try to force my way."

"Are you scared?" a reporter asked.

"Yes, I am," he answered. Then he said:

"I think the students would like me okay once I got in and they got to know me."

He said he had attended the all-Negro Horace Mann high school, where he has an A average.

"I guess they're not going to let me through," he said, as the militiamen continued to block his path.

The Negro girl, who had come earlier, sat on a bus bench. She seemed in a state of shock. A white woman, Mrs. Grace Lorch, walked over to comfort her.

"What are you doing, you nigger lover?" Mrs. Lorch was asked. "You stay away from that girl."

"She's scared," Mrs. Lorch said. "She's just a little girl." She appealed to the men and women around her.

"Why don't you calm down?" she asked. "I'm not here to fight with you. Six months from now you'll be ashamed at what you're doing."

"Go home, you're just one of them," Mrs. Lorch was told.

She escorted the Negro student to the other side of the street, but the crowd followed.

"Won't somebody please call a taxi?" she pleaded. She was met with hoot calls and jeers.

Finally, after being jostled by the crowd, she worked her way to the street corner, and the two boarded a bus.

Seven other Negro students tried to get into the school. They came together, accompanied by four white ministers. Dunbar Ogden, president of the greater Little Rock Ministerial Association acted as spokesman for the group.

"Sorry, we cannot admit Negro students," the officers of the militia told them.

The crowd began to disperse slowly. Many of the students who had waited outside the school building to see whether the Negroes would enter, started to go into school. They had said if the Negroes went in they would go out.

At his interview Governor Faubus said that the troops, under the direction of Maj. Gen. Sherman T. Clinger, had been instructed to keep Negroes out of the white school. He did this, the Governor said, to preserve order and prevent violence. He did not consider himself in contempt of court.

The guards will remain on duty until all danger of violence has ended, he said. Just how long that would be could not be determined, he added.

Governor Faubus belittled the prospect of a State-Federal conflict over authority.

"I'm not defying the Federal court order," he insisted. "I'm merely carrying out my obligation to preserve the peace."

Integration can take place in Little Rock, he said, when and if a majority of the people want mixed classes. He said he was seeking "the most peace for the most people."

Governor Faubus said that his order to keep Negroes out was based on the situation as it now existed.

Two truck loads of National Guardsmen surrounded the Governor's Mansion late this afternoon. The immediate reason for this move was not apparent. The Governor was not available for comment.

At the end of his news conference Governor Faubus warned the newsmen and photographers not to try to incite the crowd to make news. He said that several instances had been reported to him of newsreel men going out of their way to create news. The newsmen denied this.

Seven Negro students who had been denied admission went to Mr. Cobb's office to complain of their treatment. They were referred to the Federal Bureau of Investigation under direction of Joseph J. Casper, special agent.

During the day sixteen ministers of Little Rock issued a statement strongly protesting the action of Governor Faubus in calling out the troops. The ministers appealed to the citizens to maintain peace.

Little Rock Faces Showdown Today Over Integration

BY BENJAMIN FINE | SEPT. 7, 1957

LITTLE ROCK, ARK., SEPT. 6 — The tense integration issue will reach a showdown here tomorrow.

The showdown will come in Federal District Court when Judge Ronald N. Davies hears a petition from the Board of Education for a delay in admitting Negro students to white schools. National Guard troops barring Negroes from Central High School on orders from the Governor have created conditions that make it impossible to integrate now, the board said.

Meanwhile, Gov. Orval E. Faubus sent a telegram to President Eisenhower. It was interpreted as a polite no to the President's request for cooperation with a Federal court order to integrate the schools. The Governor explained his position and promised to uphold both state and Federal Constitutions. He gave no indication, however, that he would withdraw the troops.

CROWD IS SMALLER

On the fourth morning since schools opened here Tuesday the picture at the Central High School was much as it had been from the start. The crowd of segregationists in front of the school grounds was somewhat smaller. Many shouted insults at photographers and reporters urging them to "go home where you belong."

One hundred armed troops from units of the National Air Guard were on duty. No Negroes sought to enter today. The nine who had tried to do so Wednesday were turned back.

Six University of Minnesota students traveling by automobile to New Orleans almost started a riot here when one of the young men was believed to be carrying a knife. Three of the students were arrested by the soldiers, but later released.

A more serious incident was the disclosure by Mayor Woodrow W. Mann, who is opposed to the presence of troops at the school, that a cross had been burned in the yard of his home.

Governor Faubus' telegram to the President was in answer to the President's request for cooperation with Federal authorities. The Governor held his ground.

The Governor told the President that he was ready to give evidence that caused him to call out the National Guard Monday night. The troops have been used to prevent Negro students from entering the white high school, even though these students had the approval of the Board of Education to attend this school.

In his message to Governor Faubus late yesterday, President Eisenhower urged the state official to cooperate with the Federal court order to integrate the school. The President said he would use whatever legal means might be necessary to uphold the Constitution.

In a telegram of less than a hundred words, Governor Faubus said that he, too, would uphold the Federal Constitution. He insisted, however, that the National Guard had been called out to prevent violence rather than to block the court order on integration.

The guards are to remain. And the Negro students will be kept out.

Governor Faubus wired President Eisenhower:

"Thank you for your telegram in reply to my appeal for your understanding and cooperation in connection with my effort to preserve the public peace and good order in this community.

"I have notified the United States District Attorney and the F. B. I. that my personal counsel, William J. Smith, and the director or the Arkansas State Police, Herman Lindsey, are available to discuss certain evidence upon which I acted to preserve the public peace, I shall cooperate in upholding the Constitutions of Arkansas and the nation."

The statement was released to the press by Claude Carpenter, an aide to the Governor. The whereabouts of Governor Faubus has not been learned. He has not met with newsmen since his last conference on Wednesday morning. The Governor's mansion is still guarded by the state police.

The state and Federal governments are still at direct odds. The constitutional question of which has the sovereignty over the other will have to be solved before the integration issue here is settled.

NEGROES NOT ATTENDING SCHOOL

It was learned that the nine Negro students were not attending any school at present. They have been assigned places at Central High, the white school, and therefore not attending Horace Mann, the Negro school. Until the integration issue is decided, these students will be carried on the Central High rolls but will be absent.

"It's a pity that they must lose part of their education," a highly placed school official said. "If the issue is not settled soon these youngsters will be handicapped and their grades will suffer. They are not to blame. The Negroes are caught in the middle of a state-Federal conflict."

One of the nine Negroes, 15-year-old Terrance Roberts, is a straight A student. He is eager to continue with his schooling so that he can prepare for college.

"No one urged me to go to a white school," he said. "I just feel that Central is a better school than Horace Mann."

Since they are not "truants" in the traditional sense, no official action will be taken about their absences.

"But you can't make up the lost time," a board official said. "It's not fair to keep these youngsters dangling this way."

The gathering this morning brought out the usual amount of jeering, catcalls and shouts of "keep the niggers out."

Reporters and photographers were still jeered by the men and women who start to congregate at 6 o'clock in the morning and remain until the noon hour. After a bristling attack on mixed schools a well-dressed man said:

"The niggers are damn animals anyway. They hibernate like rats.

Four of the nine students walking along the sidewalk as Arkansas National Guardsmen turn them away from entering Central High School.

The only one behind bringing niggers to our schools are the white trash like Blossom" [Virgil T. Blossom, Superintendent of Schools.]

"Would you care to give me your name for the story?" this reporter asked.

The heavy-set speaker replied in anger: "I won't give you anything but a black eye."

However, more students today began to speak up in favor of letting the Negro children come into their schools.

"We don't need troops here," 15-year-old Hansdieter Bueller, a sophomore, said. "They are supposed to keep the peace but they push us around too much. If I want to stand on the sidewalk and look at somebody the guards push us back."

As for going to school with Negroes, young Hansdieter said: "It wouldn't bother me as long as they kept to themselves. I don't hold a grudge against them."

Several members of the crowd walked over while this interview was taking place. An elderly gray-haired woman who declined to give her name, cried out: "Hey kid, why don't you keep quiet?"

"Because I don't want to," he retorted. "It's a free country, lady."

Another young student broke in earnestly: "I'm not for integration really but if it comes I'll take it. The thing that hurts me is the way that some of these people talk. Most of the fellows say they don't want niggers around. But if the troops weren't here and they came in nothing would happen to them."

The newsmen, now swelled to a group of more than sixty, kept out of trouble today. They were admonished yesterday by Maj. Gen. Sherman T. Clinger to avoid any activity that might be interpreted as "inciting to riot." Under this definition, any reporter who began an interview with one or two students and found himself surrounded by several dozen others might be liable for arrest or might be barred from the school grounds.

On several occasions when a reporter stopped to talk with members of the crowd, and it began to look as though it would get out of hand, an officer would come to "break it up."

The crowd became excited when someone yelled: "There's a man with a knife." Lieut. Col. Marion Johnson, second in command, found a man with a camera over his shoulder who did have what looked like a five-inch knife in his hip pocket. He was immediately escorted from the grounds followed by a crowd of curious persons.

Later it was learned that the arrested person was one of six University of Minnesota students, traveling by auto to New Orleans as part of their vacation before college opened. They had heard about the integration conflict and had stopped by "just to see what was taking place."

THREE TAKEN INTO CUSTODY

The suspicious guardsmen took three of the six students into custody when the young men began to argue with the mob. Cries of "Go home, this place is for white men only," were answered by the students with "This is America, isn't it?" As the crowd gathered, the troops evidently decided that this came under the definition of "inciting to riot."

Finally all six were brought to the police headquarters. The man with the knife, identified as Murray Gallinson, said he had bought the knife as a souvenir on the trip that he and his friends were taking. The boy said that they were on this sightseeing tour to see this part of the country. After about an hour the state police captain, Alan Templeton, ordered all released. They immediately continued on their way to New Orleans.

Mayor Mann found the cross burning in his yard. With the aid of a neighbor, the flames were extinguished. A police car took the smoldering remains away.

The Mayor charged that this was one of the manufactured incidents being planned to give the Governor an excuse to keep the troops in this city.

He wired Governor Faubus asking that he give the people of this state evidence of possible racial violence instead of running off and hiding. (He referred to the fact that the Governor has not been available for the last two days).

N.A.A.C.P. TO OPPOSE PLEA

The board officials, superintendent of schools and other authorities are scheduled to attend tomorrow's hearing before Judge Davies. Mrs. Daisy Bates, president of the Arkansas Chapter of the National Association for the Advancement of Colored People, said that lawyers of the organization would oppose the petition asking for a delay in the integration program.

United States Attorney Osro Cobb announced that an interim report of existing conditions has been given Judge Davies in accordance with a request for a "full, thorough and complete investigation."

Regardless of what happens tomorrow, peace is not yet in sight for this tense city. General Clinger revealed that orders are already out for full strength patrols at the high school on Monday morning. Over the week-end a token force of fifteen troops will keep guard. But starting Monday morning from 100 to 250 National Guardsmen, fully armed, will be on duty.

General Clinger said he had ordered the Morrilton Guard unit to report. It will relieve the Air Guard troops now stationed at the school.

FAUBUS TO BE ON TV

Governor Faubus will be questioned by a panel of newsmen tomorrow afternoon on a television program originating in Little Rock.

Michael Foster, vice president of the American Broadcasting Company, said early today that the Governor had agreed to appear live on the "Open Hearing" program from 5:30 to 6 o'clock tomorrow. John Secondari, ABC Chief of the Washington Bureau, will be moderator of the program to be carried by the entire network from KATV in Little Rock. The New York outlet is WABC-TV, Channel 7.

Students Unhurt

BY BENJAMIN FINE | SEPT. 24, 1957

LITTLE ROCK, ARK., SEPT. 23 — A mob of belligerent, shrieking and hysterical demonstrators forced the withdrawal today of nine Negro students from Central High School here.

Despite a heavy turnout of local and state police to see that the Negroes were not molested in Little Rock's newest attempt to integrate the high school, city authorities bowed to the fury of about 1,000 white supremacists. They ordered the Negro students to leave the school about noon. The integration attempt had lasted 3 hours 13 minutes.

While fringe fights broke out, and several persons were "roughed up" by irate segregationists, the mob shouted insults and obscenities against the "niggers" and "nigger lovers." Groups of white students who had walked out of the school after the nine Negroes entered chanted: "Two, four, six, eight, we ain't gonna integrate."

STUDENTS DENY VIOLENCE

Reports that some of the Negro youngsters had been attacked inside the school by white students were denied by the Negro students.

One of them said that he thought he had been pushed once, but that was apparently the extent of activities within classes.

There was uncertainty about what the Negro students would do tomorrow. Mrs. L. C. Bates, president of the Arkansas branch of the National Association for the Advancement of Colored People, said that "a little more assurance" than President Eisenhower had given in his proclamation would be necessary before the Negroes would go back to school.

Virgil T. Blossom, Superintendent of Schools, said that authorities were working on the assumption that the Negroes would not show up for classes tomorrow.

Meanwhile, at midnight, Little Rock still showed signs of tense-ness. Several fist fights between Negroes and whites were reported by the police. Two Negroes who were in a car being chased by the police were injured when the automobile crashed off the highway.

Police squad cars patrolled the city's streets throughout the night, ready to break up any large groups and prevent racial violence if it developed. The authorities do not believe that in this city of 117,000 persons, of which 25 per cent are Negroes, a race riot will occur, but every precaution was being taken.

The police tonight intercepted a caravan of fifty to 100 cars near a Little Rock factory. Occupants of the cars, mostly men and youths, were dispersed easily by the police.

Lieut. Gov. Nathan Gordon, Acting Governor, called on the people of Little Rock to be calm and engage in no acts of violence.

Out of more than 1,900 students enrolled in Central High School, about 300 left classes in the first hour of the attempted integration. The school superintendent said that about 450 students had either left the building or were absent this morning. Many of them, it is believed, withdrew or stayed away to avoid trouble.

The Negroes were escorted safely through the mob by the police and taken to their homes without injury.

Mayor Woodrow Wilson Mann charged that the violence outside the school had been stirred up by plan and "bore all the marks of the professional agitators." He said that detailed information on the events of the day would be turned over to the Department of Justice for what-ever action the Federal Government considered warranted.

"The names of individuals who were ringleaders of this incitement will be turned over to the Federal Bureau of Investigation," the Mayor declared.

Many of those who milled in front of the school today were from out of town, some from communities 200 miles distant. It was noted that one of those in the crowd of demonstrators was Jimmy Karam, Athletic Commissioner for the state and a close friend of the Governor.

N. A. A. C. P. 'GRATIFIED'

President Eisenhower's proclamation, pledging to use the full power of the United States, including force if necessary, to carry out the orders of Federal Judge Ronald N. Davies for integration of the school, was welcomed by officials of the National Association for the Advancement of Colored People here. They termed it "gratifying and a step forward."

Mrs. Bates had declared earlier that the Negro youngsters "will not be out there again until they have the assurance of the President of the United States that they will be protected from the mob."

Mrs. Bates said after the proclamation:

"I want to be absolutely sure that they will be protected and how before they [the students] will be advised to return.

"I hope that the immediate and wholehearted compliance of all the citizens with the existing court decrees, assuring these youngsters of nonsegregated education, will take place in our community."

She said that the Negro students who went into the school today were surprised when they were withdrawn from their classes. They felt that they had been treated kindly by the white students.

9 STUDENTS SHOW UP

Mr. Blossom, in his statement tonight, said he understood the Negro students did not plan to return to school tomorrow. He declared, however, that the Negroes were still enrolled in the school and were still eligible to enter if they wished.

Ten Negro students had been selected to enter classes at Central High, and nine of them — six girls and three boys — showed up for the test today. They were taken into the school through another entrance, quietly and apparently unnoticed by most of the demonstrators, who were shouting from across the barricades in front of the school.

Several persons suffered minor injuries in the clashes. Francis Miller, a photographer for Life magazine, was knocked down and struck in the face. Later two other Life representatives were attacked.

Another newsman, Alex Wilson, a Negro, representing a Memphis, Tenn., Negro newspaper, was beaten and kicked by members of the mob. It was during this incident that the nine Negro students were driven on to the campus of the high school and were escorted through a side door into the building.

While the crowd was still milling in front of the high school, some white students went to a nearby Catholic school for Negroes, St. Bartholomew's, and went after a group of students. The students ducked inside the building and escaped injury.

Later, three Negroes attacked a 16-year-old white boy, James Mill, as he was walking home. Lou Ann Montgomery, 15, a sophomore at Central High, said that two Negro men stopped her while she was going home for lunch and cut her right hand "with what looked like a piece of a broken whisky bottle."

24 ARE ARRESTED

During the day, the police seized twenty-four men and women in front of the Central High School for disturbing the peace and resisting arrest. Many of those arrested grappled with the police and had to be carried forcibly away. Four policeman carried one struggling man to the patrol car, swinging him by his hands and feet, before he was finally subdued.

"Leave that man alone," the mob shouted, trying to break through the barriers. The police held fast.

Several women, shrieking and screaming, also were carried away. As one woman was placed into the patrol wagon, a man shrieked and tried to get by the police line. He yelled, "That's my wife."

The local authorities took no action today to get National Guard units to the scene. Mr. Gordon had promised to call out Guardsmen if city officials requested them. The National Guard had been stationed at the school from Sept. 3 until last Friday, during which period they barred Negroes from entering the school. But the military units were withdrawn Friday in conformity with Judge Davies's order.

Tri-State Defender reporter Alex Wilson is shoved by an angry mob of white people near Central High School. Moments later, the man at far left jumped him. Besides Mr. Wilson, three other Negro newsmen were manhandled.

The National Guard had been stationed at the school by Gov. Orval E. Faubus to "prevent violence" after the Federal Court had approved a plan for integration. When Governor Faubus, who is now in Sea Island, Ga., attending the Southern Governors Conference, ordered the troops withdrawn on Friday he advised the Negro students not to try to enter the school, until a "cooling-off" period had passed.

STREET BARRICADED

For a time this morning it appeared as though integration would take place smoothly in this city of 102,213 population. A few persons arrived at the high school by 6 o'clock. By 7, with the sun just beginning to break through the clouds, only 100 or so had gathered at both ends of the street leading to the two-lock-long school. Wooden barricades, placed on both ends of the street, stopped them at those points.

Eighty members of the local police force, some on motorcycles and in squad cars, but most on foot, were on the schools grounds or in the vicinity. Fifty state troopers were in the area, ready to help if needed.

At 8 o'clock it was evident that the violence that Governor Faubus had predicted would take place. By this time some 500 persons had gathered. They appeared in a fighting mood.

"The niggers won't get in," members of the crowd said, time and again.

At 8:45 the school buzzer could be dimly heard. School was in session.

"Where are the niggers?" one person asked another. "Let them try to get in …"

"We'll lynch them all," several yelled.

"Sure, and all you Yankee newspaper men with them," a gravel-voiced man shouted. This was met with a howl of approval.

The police tried to keep the crowd off the street. The surging angry mob kept pushing forward.

"Please keep back, step back," the police said politely at first, then with more authority.

"Don't you dare lay your hands on me," one woman screamed as a police officer asked her to move away.

"Lady," he pleaded, "I'm not going to touch you. I'm just doing my duty."

Suddenly a yell went up.

"There they are, they're coming," came a shout.

The crowd rushed after four men who turned out to be Negro newspaper men. They were manhandled by the crowd, but managed to escape.

A man yelled:

"Look, they're going into our school."

Six girls and three boys crossed over into the school yard. They had arrived in two automobiles and had driven to the side of the school. Mrs. Bates accompanied them.

Slowly, almost as though they were entering a normal classroom on a normal school day, the students walked toward the side door of the school. The boys, in open shirts, the girls, in bobbysox, joked and chatted among themselves. They carried armfuls of textbooks.

The crowd now let out a roar of rage. "They've gone in," a man shouted.

"Oh, God," said a woman, "the niggers are in school."

A group of six girls, dressed in skirts and sweaters, hair in ponytails, started to shriek and wail.

"The niggers are in our school," they howled hysterically.

One of them jumped up and down on the sidewalk, waving her arms toward her classmates in the school who were looking out of the windows, and screamed over and over again:

"Come on out, come on out."

Tears flowed down her face, her body shook in uncontrollable spasms.

Three of her classmates grew hysterical, and threw their arms around each other. They began dancing up and down.

"The niggers are in," they shrieked, "come on out of the school. Don't stay there with the niggers. Come on out. Come on..."

Hysteria swept from the shrieking girls to members of the crowd. Women cried hysterically, tears running down their faces.

"I'm going to get the niggers out," said Mrs. Clyde Thomason, recording secretary of the Mothers League of Central High, a segregationist group.

She started toward the school. Two policemen blocked her way.

"Please go back on the sidewalk," one begged quietly.

"Go on and hit me, just go and hit me," Mrs. Thomason, who had been enjoined by Judge Davies not to interfere with the integration program, said. She became hysterical.

A man walked over to the policemen who were struggling to restrain Mrs. Thomason.

"This is my wife, officer," he said. "I'll take her with me."

An elderly man jumped upon the barricade.

"Let's go over the top," he shouted. "Who's going over with me?"

"We'll all go," the crowd yelled.

Over the wooden barricade they went. A dozen policemen stood in the way. Slowly the crowd gave way.

The police were taunted by the mob, well out of hand by now. Instead of tapering off, as it had at previous morning demonstrations, the crowd grew in numbers. By 10 o'clock it had grown to about 1,000.

"Turn in your badge," the crowd yelled at the police.

One of the policemen said, apologetically:

"I'm only doing my duty. If I didn't I'd lose my job."

TAKES OFF BADGE

Another one, Thomas Dunaway, took off his badge and walked away.

"Hurray! hurray!" the crowd cheered.

"He's the only white man on the force," a young man in a plaid shirt shouted.

"Let's pass the hat around," some one suggested.

In a moment several persons went through the crowd, collecting money. Dollar bills were tossed into the hat. It was estimated that about $200 had been collected for the policeman who gave up his badge.

The men and women, augmented by students, surged over the "off limits" line and spread into the street facing the school grounds.

A dozen state troopers, with service revolvers and Sam Browne belts, were rushed to the school grounds. For a time it appeared as though the local police would be completed overwhelmed by the angry crowd.

"Come on out of school, come on out, the niggers are in there," the crowd yelled.

Four girls slowly walked down the wide steps of the high school.

A tremendous cheer echoed through the crowd.

"They're coming out," was shouted time and again.

Soon a group of six left. The students began to leave the school at more frequent intervals. At first the police did not permit adults to enter the school. They were acting under order of Mr. Blossom.

"I'm going to get my child," one parent said defiantly.

"Sorry, you'll stay right here," the policeman answered.

Quickly this order changed. One by one, mothers and fathers walked up the school steps, and then returned with their children. Each time a student walked out of the school the cheers increased.

"Mother, come and get me," a girl telephoned. "They're fighting something awful here inside the school."

By 12 o'clock the mob had reached its greatest strength, and by now completely ignored the local police. The crowd remained behind the barricade, but it did not maintain order there. Several newsmen were attacked and beaten. A Negro reporter was kicked and manhandled.

Threats, jeers, and insults became more ominous.

"Let's rush the police," a ringleader shouted. "They can't stop us."

At noon the police received this message on their shortwave radios:

"This is the Mayor. Tell Principal Jess Matthews [of Central High] that the Negroes have been withdrawn. Tell Mr. Matthews to announce that to the student body. I've talked with Virgil Blossom and the Negroes have been withdrawn."

NEGROES WITHDRAWN

At 12:14 Lieut. Carl Jackson of the Little Rock police force stood on the school grounds facing the crowd. Over a loudspeaker set up on the sidewalk in front of the school the officer said:

"The Negroes have been withdrawn from school."

"We don't believe you," the crowd yelled back, "That's just a pack of lies."

"Is there anyone whom you would believe?" he asked.

"I saw a nigger standing in the doorway just now," a woman yelled.

"Let's go in and see," another shouted.

"If you have any one person in the crowd you believe, they can go in and see, then report to you," Lieutenant Jackson said.

Mrs. Allen Thevenet of the Mothers League of Central High School, stepped forward across the street.

"Will you accept Mrs. Thevenet's word?" the lieutenant asked. The crowd gave a reluctant approval.

Accompanied by a policeman, Mrs. Thevenet went into the school. On her return she came to the loudspeaker and said:

"We went through every room in the school and there was no niggers there."

"How do we know they ain't hiding some place in the school?" a man shouted.

AFRAID TO LEAVE

Lieutenant Jackson called for Mr. Matthews. He too reassured the crowd with the statement:

"The Negroes have been withdrawn from school."

"We don't believe you," the mob shouted. The principal was loudly booed.

"Are they coming back after dinner?" the crowd asked the lieutenant.

"No," he said.

The Negro students, meantime, had been taken out through a side door, and escorted in two police cars to their homes. Despite the rumors that had been flying through the crowd that the students "had been beat up," they were not molested while in school.

"They were surprised when they were told to leave at noontime," Mrs. Bates said later.

"Nothing much happened at all," Thelma Mothershed, one of the nine Negro students, said.

"Nothing really happened," agreed Terrance Roberts, 16. "We went to classes as scheduled. After the third period we were taken out and driven home. Some school officials came in to see us."

He added: "I was pushed once but I wasn't hit. It was quiet after we got into our classes. A few white students walked out."

Another of the girls, Elizabeth Ann Eckford, 15, said:

"I was the only Negro girl in my class."

Would they want to come back?

"Yes," they agreed, "if we can come here without causing any trouble. The students will accept us once we go with them for a while."

Osro Cobb, United States Attorney, said that complaints of violations of Federal laws would receive prompt attention. He said:

"I will not hesitate to proceed criminally against provocators who conspire together and act in concert in an effort to forcibly deny rights secured to our citizens by the Constitution of the United States.

"Our grand jury is now in session and if such incidents occur while this grand jury is in session, it is possible that the matter can be presented immediately to the grand jury. In any event we will act firmly and with dispatch as the situation warrants."

Fighter for Integration

SPECIAL TO THE NEW YORK TIMES | SEPT. 24, 1957

Daisy Getson Bates wants more assurance.

LITTLE ROCK, SEPT. 23 — The woman who has been on the front line in this city's turbulent school integration fight hardly looks the part. Five foot three inches tall, weighing 125 pounds, Mrs. Lucius Christopher Bates resembles a college student or a young school teacher more than a leader whose life is constantly threatened. For the last five years Mrs. Bates has been president of the Arkansas Branch of the National Association for the Advancement of Colored People. As a result, she has borne the brunt of the integration dispute here. When Gov. Orval E. Faubus on Sept. 2 ordered the National Guard to Central High School, Mrs. Bates immediately went into action — and she has not stopped since.

This morning, when nine Negro students entered Central High, breaking the color line in Little Rock School for the first time, Mrs. Bates rode to school with them. After they entered, she remained near the school for some time, to be certain that nothing happened to them.

After a mob forced school authorities to withdraw the Negro students, Mrs. Bates said that they would not go back until the President assured their safety.

WANTS MORE ASSURANCE

Informed of the President's threat to use force to carry out integration, Mrs. Bates said she wanted a little more assurance on protection before she advised the students to return to the school.

This has not been an easy time for Mrs. Bates. For the past three weeks she has been vilified, abused, threatened and intimidated. Her phone rings constantly, day and night. Most of the callers do not give their names, but spit warnings at her. "We'll kill you, you black nigger," some say.

The Bateses have an 11-year old adopted son, Clyde. He, too, has been threatened.

"I'm not worried about myself," Mrs. Bates says, "but I'm frightened sick about Clyde."

Since the threats and warnings have started, the Bateses have installed floodlights around their house. They shine all night. Friends take turns staying up at the house throughout the night.

Mrs. Bates was born Daisy Getson thirty-eight years ago in Hutting, in the southeast section of Arkansas. She attended schools there and went to college for two years. Her father, a lumber grader at a sawmill, made better than average wages. As a child Daisy knew nothing of racial differences: at 6 her best friend was Janie, a white girl in the neighborhood.

Then one day her mother sent her to a butcher shop to get a pound of pork chops. She went to the store and said: "I want a pound of center-cut pork chops, please." Just then several white persons came in.

"The butcher turned away from me and waited on the others," she recalls. "He ignored me for thirty minutes. I became angry and cried out: 'But I was here first.'

"After the others had been served the man said curtly: 'What do you want, nigger?' "

"I've never forgotten that incident," she says. "I decided I would do what I could to help my race. I don't want my boy to be hurt the way I was."

The Bateses were married in 1941. That year they founded the Arkansas State Press, a Negro weekly. It is now one of the most influential publications in the field, with a circulation of 20,000.

In the last few weeks, however, the paper has felt a growing economic boycott. Local advertising worth thousands of dollars has been withdrawn.

"I don't know how long we can keep the paper going," Mrs. Bates says.

Students Accept Negroes Calmly

BY BENJAMIN FINE | SEPT. 26, 1957

No incidents reported inside Central High during first full day of integration.

LITTLE ROCK, SEPT. 25 — The nine Negro students who entered Central High School today were not molested nor heckled by their new class-mates, they said.

They appeared for classes just after the flag-raising ceremony that signaled school was officially in session.

The nine students were driven to school in an Army station wagon. The girls wore gay-colored dresses. The boys wore open-collared sport shirts. They carried their textbooks under their arms. One boy swung his books from a strap, in traditional schoolboy manner.

Slowly, seemingly unaware of the soldiers that had made the cam-pus into an armed camp, the students climbed the long winding stairs leading to the school. On Monday, to the catcalls of a shrieking mob, they had entered through a side door.

"Look at them, going through the front door," shouted a 15-year-old boy who said he would not go to school with the Negroes. "They're pretty high and mighty, ain't they?"

SOME RESENTMENT VOICED

The only sound in answer was the click of cameras, the jockeying into position of photographers, and the scratching of pencils on pads by reporters.

Some of the persons who live in the block of houses facing the school were bitter. Some were resentful. Others simply refused to accept what they had just seen.

"This is the grimmest moment of my life," said 47-year-old Mrs. L. G. Nunley. She sat with two women and three young children on the porch of her house. "I went to that school. My three daughters went. But my four grandchildren won't go."

The others nodded in sympathy as she continued: "The Communists are behind this. My grandmother told me forty years ago this would come if we had a Republican President."

"I didn't sleep a wink last night," the other woman said. "I wish I could tell you what's inside me right now."

From all appearances, inside the school all was superficially calm. Twenty-four paratroopers were assigned to keep order, to see that no one interfered with the court injunction on integration that had been the cause of all this Federal action.

Before the Negro students had arrived Maj. Gen. Edwin A. Walker, in charge of the Military District in Arkansas, and now running "Operation Integration" spoke to the students at a special assembly program.

"You have nothing to fear from my soldiers," he said. "No one will interfere with your coming, going or your peaceful pursuit of your studies."

Then he added: "Those who interfere or disrupt the proper administration of the school will be removed by the soldiers on duty and turned over to the local police."

Actually, there was not much in the way of education today. The troops were too great a distraction. The Negro students in the classrooms were a novelty. And from time to time groups of students threw down their books and walked out of the school. Some of them chanted sing-song words that went "two four six eight, we don't want to integrate."

Many classes were half empty. Segregationist leaders had called for a student boycott. It was partly successful. Seven hundred and fifty of the 2,000 students remained away. However, the school officials thought that this might have been from fear rather than from sympathy with the boycott movement. The next few days will tell the tale.

ABOUT 50 QUIT SCHOOL

However, no mass exodus took place today. At most, fifty boys and girls walked out. Two boys in black leather jackets were escorted from the school by a paratrooper.

"Why did they throw you out?" they were asked, as they were marched off the premises.

"We ain't talking," came the reply. Then one said: "We didn't take a clip at the nigger, but we would have if we had found him."

A tense uneasiness existed in the school. The teachers tried to carry on as best they could.

"Everything seems to be in normal condition and education is proceeding under the present conditions," said Jess Matthews, the principal.

Suddenly, over the school intercom, came the terse announcement: "Prepare for fire drill."

The police had received two threats that Central High would be bombed. The first was ignored. But the recent dynamiting at Nashville was not completely forgotten. The school officials thought that it was best to play it safe and that the school could be easily emptied through the ruse of a fire drill.

The students left the classrooms and assembled in front of the school. They chanted joked and laughed. The fire drill began at 11:05 A. M. Thirty minutes later the "all clear" signal was issued.

NEGROES JOIN CLASSMATES

The nine Negro students came out with their classmates. Some chatted with their newly found white classmates. Minnie Brown 16, a junior, walked beside a blond blue-eyed girl. The two appeared to be enjoying themselves together.

"Are you making any friends Minnie?" a reporter asked.

"Yes I am," she replied pleasantly. "Quite a few, indeed."

"If the parents would just go home and leave us be," a senior who wants to go into research said, "we'd work this thing out for ourselves."

One of the teachers, who hushed her thirty-eight youngsters so that she could be heard said earnestly:

"The Negro students seem to be getting along very well with other students. There is no trouble in the school now."

"It is just the idea of going to school with colored kids that's hard to take at first," a boy of 17 remarked. "Once you get used to the idea it's not bad."

There is considerable pressure from segregationist groups to expand the boycott.

"I had half a dozen calls last night from people telling me not to show up today," a 16-year-old girl said. "They told me there'd be trouble in school that it wouldn't be safe."

"You know, this is funny," said another girl, a native of Little Rock. "We are called nigger-lovers just because we go to school with the colored kids."

Some of those that objected to the nine students used the time honored cliches that had been heard each morning here for the last three weeks.

"I'm not going to school with niggers," said Coy Vance, 17, a senior, who's planning to be a doctor, "because they are inferior to us. If I catch one I'll chase him out of the school."

And his 16-year-old sister, Bonnie, added: "If they didn't have soldiers in the halls the niggers would get murdered."

Another senior, Tommy Dunn, who is undecided whether to be an actor or a singer, refused to go to school today. He was vehement in his reasons why: "I just won't go with niggers," he said. "I think that if they get chased in the halls enough they will leave by themselves. Don't they know we don't want them?"

Not everyone had that view. During the luncheon period, one of the three Negro boys sat by himself eating his sandwich and sipping a glass of milk. A white boy and girl who sat down to eat not far away, saw the lonely lad.

"Won't you join us?" the white boy asked.

The Negro grinned broadly. He arose with enthusiasm, and said: "Gee, thanks, I'd love to."

The two white students and the Negro student ate together and chatted in a friendly manner.

"I'm sure that everything will work out all right," said Mrs. L. C. Bates, president of the Arkansas branch of the National Association for the Advancement of Colored People. "We must all be patient."

The Negro students agreed. They did not experience any real trouble during their first day, despite the threats of those who walked out or those who boycotted the integrated classes.

"This was just like any other school day," said Gloria Ray, 16, a junior, one of the nine Negro students. "My classmates were very nice to me. I recited some, too. I made a few new friends."

That was the general attitude. Terrence Roberts, 16, a senior, said that "everyone acted nice." He added: "I didn't have any trouble. I think, though, that my studies will be harder than they were at Horace Mann [a Negro high school he had attended]. But I'm sure I'll get along."

Terrence is a straight-A student and plans to go to college.

AN UNPLEASANT INCIDENT

Melba Pattillo, 15, a junior, who wants to go on the stage as an entertainer, had only one unpleasant experience.

"When I got to my English class," she said, "one boy jumped to his feet and began to talk. He told the others to walk out with him because a 'nigger' was in their class. He kept talking and talking, but no one listened. The teacher told him to leave the room.

"The boy started for the door and shouted: 'Who's going with me?' No one did. So he said in disgust, 'chicken!' and left.

"I had a real nice day."

To her surprise, many of the white students not only chatted with her, but also asked her to join them at the cafeteria table. Melba has an invitation to join several white girls tomorrow at the school lunchroom.

HITS TWO HOME RUNS

She was popular in the physical education class, too. "I hit two home runs in the ball game," she added. "I'm going to get along here just fine."

Melba spent three hours and thirteen minutes in Central High School on Monday.

"It wasn't too good then," she remarked, "One of the white girls slapped my face hard. I don't know why. I didn't do anything to her."

Sixteen-year-old Thelma Mothershed, who plans to be an elementary school teacher, agreed with her Negro classmates that "everyone was nice."

"I like Central better than Horace Mann," she said, "even though I'll have to work harder. I'm not afraid of what will happen after the troops leave. I'm sure that everything will calm down after awhile.

"When they find out that we are nice, and that we want to be friends, the white students will accept us."

"Things would be better if only the grown-ups wouldn't mix in," said Ernest Green, 16, whose ambition is to get a college education. "The kids have nothing against us. They hear bad things about us from their parents."

The Negro students are confident that they can win the fight against race prejudice. "We just want to be friends," they say. "We aren't mad at anybody."

9 in Little Rock Leave Unguarded

BY PHILIP BENJAMIN | OCT. 24, 1957

LITTLE ROCK, ARK., OCT. 23 — Nine Negro students attending Central High School walked out of the school after classes today without a military escort.

It was the first time this had happened since Sept. 25, when, under President Eisenhower's order, troops of the 101st Airborne Infantry had begun providing a heavy guard for the Negroes to and from the school.

A spokesman for the headquarters of Maj. Gen. Edwin A. Walker, who commands Federal troops in Arkansas, said tonight that the removal of the troop escort was "a new policy instituted today." The spokesman said it was "just another step" in efforts by the Army to reduce its role at the school.

No advance notice of the move had been given by the Army.

ESCORTED INTO SCHOOL

For the last two weeks a National Guard officer had accompanied the Negro students to and from the school entrance. A Guard officer had escorted the students into the school this morning.

Although no military personnel accompanied the Negro students from the school to the sidewalk this afternoon, the Army continued to provide transportation for them. As usual, the Negro students climbed into an Army station wagon and were driven to their homes, an Army jeep preceding the station wagon.

The Army declined to say specifically whether the new policy also covered the arrival of the Negroes at the school in the morning. But the spokesman indicated that the removal of a troop escort applied both ways.

Four National Guard soldiers continued to patrol the sidewalk in front of the school. The Army said that nine paratroopers of the 101st

Airborne Infantry and twenty-one National Guardsmen were still on duty inside the school.

Today, for the first time in two weeks, all nine Negro students attended classes at Central High School. School officials reported that 501 students had stayed out today, mostly because of illness. The school has a total enrollment of 1,963.

FAUBUS 'NOT READY'

Before the withdrawal of the Negro students' escort, Gov. Orval E. Faubus said today that he was not ready to accept the National Guard back from Federal service.

He said there was a "serious question" whether the defederalized troops were any longer in the National Guard.

Mr. Faubus cited the case of the Arkansas National Guard after World War II and after the Korean conflict. He said the Guard troops then "were discharged and returned to civilian status and the National Guard had to be re-created."

The National Guard was federalized by President Eisenhower on Sept. 24. He rushed troops of the 101st Airborne Infantry Division to Little Rock on the same day to prevent mobs from hindering the court-ordered racial integration of Central High School.

Previously Mr. Faubus had used the National Guard to keep nine Negro students from entering the school. He said he did so to preserve order.

While the entire National Guard, composed of approximately 10,500 men, had been placed on Federal service by President Eisenhower, relatively few troops have been physically on duty. Only about 1,500 have been in uniform at any one time and some of these have been replaced from time to time. Most Guardsmen have remained at their civilian occupations, reporting twice a day to their unit headquarters and drawing full active duty pay.

Little Rock Girl Sees More Strife

BY THE NEW YORK TIMES | FEB. 23, 1958

A NEGRO STUDENT expelled from Central High School at Little Rock, Ark., said yesterday that Negro pupils were continually being harassed by white students there. As a result, she said, integration is being strained to the breaking point.

The student, Minnijean Brown, arrived in New York from Little Rock with her mother to enroll as a scholarship student at the private New Lincoln School, 31 West 110th Street. She was received by a representative of the school and about fifty delegates of city youth councils and high schools.

The 16-year-old girl said she had been expelled for violating an agreement with school authorities by the Negro students not to retaliate to harassment from other pupils.

Asked whether she believed the eight remaining Negro students would be able to maintain a passive acceptance, Miss Brown said:

"Things cannot go on as they are. I'm praying for the other kids, but I don't think they are going to stand it."

She said, however, that she had not given up hope that integration would work out successfully at Little Rock.

Miss Brown's expulsion came after several suspensions for run-ins with white students.

"I took abuse from them. I was kicked twice. I was called all kinds of terrible names, but I always walked away and I laughed at it. But finally, I couldn't."

Miss Brown described the final incident that led to her ouster in a soft, high-pitched voice. Her mother, Mrs. Imogene Brown, was at her side during the news conference at La Guardia Airport.

She said a white girl had followed her in a corridor of the school "calling me all kinds of unmentionable names."

"I was taught not to use bad language, but after so much complications I got mad," Miss Brown said. "I just let go and called her white trash."

She said that despite her expulsion she felt "no bitterness whatsoever."

Miss Brown said, however, that she had not given up hope that the integration program would work out successfully at Little Rock.

"I think it will come out alright," she said. "At least, I hope so."

She said that she "wished with all my heart" that she could have continued at Central High, but that she was looking forward to New Lincoln School.

She told reporters that she had recently changed the spelling of her name from Minnie-jean to Minnijean.

Mrs. Brown, who has three other children, said her husband, a building contractor, had had increasing difficulty getting work since the Little Rock school integration began last fall.

"I am sure that this is another form of retaliation," she said. She said she planned to return to Little Rock as soon as her daughter gets settled here.

Little Rock: More Tension Than Ever

BY GERTRUDE SAMUELS | MARCH 23, 1958

Integration at Central High School no longer makes headlines, but a hard core of segregationists has kept the issue very much alive. The real crisis may be yet to come.

LAST SEPTEMBER LITTLE ROCK was a focus of national and international attention. For about a month it was featured dramatically in newspaper headlines. In the past five months little has been reported out of Little Rock, and as a result many readers have assumed that all is calm and under control. And on the surface it would so appear.

Yet the fact is that the situation is more explosive than ever. And what is happening is a symbol of a people's great dilemma — in Little Rock in particular and the South in general.

Last September the city's school board began putting into effect its 1955 plan to desegregate the public schools gradually — admitting Negroes to senior high schools in 1957, to junior high schools in 1960, to grade schools in 1963. But state guardsmen, under orders from Gov. Orval Faubus, prevented the nine registered Negro students from entering Central High School on Sept. 4. Later that month a Federal court directed that the nine children must be admitted. And on Sept. 23 a mob of 1,000 whites fought, cursed and wept outside the school as the nine entered a side door of Central High. By noon the Negroes were removed for their safety.

Next day the President ordered the guardsmen federalized, and sent a thousand men of the 101st Airborne Division to Little Rock to rout the mob and guard the Negro students.

SINCE THAT TIME the Federal troops have been withdrawn, and only a token number of federalized National Guardsmen remain inside and outside the school. There is no mob outside the school; children enter and leave freely; this would seem to indicate serenity and order.

But, in reality, the mob has moved inside the school. A hard core of white students, known as "segregationists," operates inside the school a systematic campaign of terror and coercion. It is a well-planned program of intimidation of the decent whites — both students and educators — inside the school and among school officials.

The most recent example of its influence concerns a 16-year-old member of the segregationists — a blond girl expelled by the school for having allegedly attacked the woman vice principal physically and circulated cards bearing inflammatory legends; yet a few days later, after this girl had denounced the school and the city police over a state-wide television hook-up paid for by the adult segregationist group, she was readmitted to Central High School on her promise to observe school regulations.

For ten days this reporter has observed the atmosphere in this capital city, both in the school and outside the school, and she has attempted to find the answers to these questions:

What is going on inside the school today? What do the students and the people of Little Rock have to say about the school picture? What does it portend for youngsters here and the community? And what does it mean in terms of integration throughout the South?

Little Rock Central High School, which had its thirtieth birthday last November, is an impressive structure physically, rising like a small, regal university in yellow-bricked grandeur on spacious, landscaped grounds.

THE SCHOOL accommodates 2,000 students in 100 classrooms built on seven levels; its enormous auditorium holds the entire school population. The second level is the busiest — since most of the basic-skills classrooms are on this floor, as are also the offices of school officials, the auditorium and bookstore. Various shop-work classes, laboratories, music and art rooms, gym and lunchrooms are distributed on the other levels. The great attraction of Central is its advanced instructional and activities programs (many of which, incidentally, are not available at the all-colored Horace Mann High School).

On the day of this reporter's visit to Central High, the only observable excitement was that engendered by the basketball test-game called for that evening. Superficially, it was typical teen-age frolic spirit.

A large brown paper bag hung on a corridor wall bore the mascot slogan: "It's in the bag — a Tiger victory!" At the pep assembly, the rafters rang with the youngsters' songs and cheers, whipped up by energetic cheer-leaders and a swing band on stage: "A basket, a basket, a basket, boys. You make the basket, we'll make the noise!" (The Tigers won that night.)

AND IN THE classrooms, as one moved about the different levels of the school, normalcy seemed the pattern. In one class of some twenty youngsters, the gray-haired teacher was discussing college placement procedures. Terrence Roberts, a junior, one of the Negro children, sat among the students, sharing their quiet attention to their teacher's advice.

Down in the boys' gym, Jefferson Thomas, youngest of the three Negro boys among the group, played with the volley-ball team. The only qualification visible here was that of skill, as young Thomas dashed about with the others, catching and tossing the ball while the instructor stood by.

Particularly in a physics laboratory did one get an impression of harmony inside the classroom. Here the only senior of the Negro group, Ernest Green, who will be graduating in June, sat beside a white boy in his class, working on small motors, generators and electricity. Ernest and the white boy occasionally exchanged murmured comments on a problem, or helped each other, or looked sheepish when some idea didn't work out.

But outside the classrooms there is an all too noticeable difference in atmosphere. In the corridors, as classes were belled to change, uniformed guardsmen, singly and in pairs, moved among the students. The token number of guards, inside the school or cruising in jeeps on the outside, are estimated at thirty. In the congested corridors one senses the tension that the Negro newcomers and many others must feel.

FOR IN CONTRAST to most students, the Negroes walk alone, silently, rapidly, a little scared, looking to neither right nor left as they make for their next classes. They are watchful on the steps where several have met with "accidents." They keep their eyes peeled for the known segregationists. In the chatter and laughter of the corridors, this observer saw no white student stop to talk or smile with them.

After six months in the school, they seem as effectively isolated or ostracized as though they were in a hostile land where no one spoke their language. In the student cafeteria on the mezzanine, they sit at a small table that the white students have in effect reserved for them. No white ever sits with them.

But the situation, you discover, is not a racial issue with many of the whites inside the building.

You see that there are many among the white students, some of whom throw an expressionless look toward the hurrying Negro children as they pass, who would like to stop, say something to them, talk over homework or problems, perhaps lunch with them again — as many did on their first day of school last September — but who do not now dare to do so.

In interviews with whites, adults and students, outside the school the observer is told that the intimidation of both Negroes and whites follows two courses:

(1) With the small Negro group, the segregationists practice harassment, petty cruelties and outright violence. Over the past six months, the pattern has included numerous instances of kicking the colored children, banging them against their lockers, spitting on them, tripping them in halls, pushing them downstairs, stepping on their heels, sticking nails on their seats, and pouring soup over one of them. Name-calling is one of the least harassments today, since "nigger …

nigger… nigger…" and "nigger, go back to Africa" have become so routine a cruelty that the colored students barely react to it any more. Indeed, the only youngster who did retaliate — Minnijean Brown — was expelled, and is now attending school in New York.

(2) With the decent, law-abiding whites in the school — and they are said to be the large majority of the students and teachers — the hard-core segregationists have developed so systematic and organized a pattern of psychological warfare that it is virtually 100 per cent successful.

ONE MUST REMEMBER that Central High students are 15- to 17-year-olds, young adolescents raised in the tradition of segregation; for them not only is society segregated in fact, but segregation is morally right and correct. Observers of the past six months point out that unless they acquire a more liberal attitude on race relations by osmosis from the outside, they will not doubt the rectitude of their position.

Nevertheless, there are many decent young people who believe in law and order and fair play. But any overtures by them to the Negroes are unthinkable today. They have become cowed by the bullyings of the segregationists; and the warnings from their parents who either want their children "to stay out of trouble," or have themselves been threatened with social or economic boycott by adult segregationists. The young extremists inside the school advise them when any fraternizing is attempted.

IN SHORT, a small mob of militant segregationist students, inside the school, is in control. It is estimated at between fifty and 100 students, or less than 5 per cent of the school population. They appear to be directed by adults on the outside.

Their campaign strategy concentrates first on this individual, then on that one. Following the expulsion of Minnijean ("Big M" as she was known because of her size), 15-year-old Gloria Ray, a Negro sophomore, was handed a small, professionally printed card which read

N. A. A. C. P. leader Daisy Bates, standing, speaks with some of the nine students at her home in Little Rock, Ark., in October 1957.

"One down… eight to go," and penciled on the reverse side, "Gloria, you're next!"

Any attempt by a white student to show a sign of friendliness outside the classroom and away from the teachers' supervision results in telephone threats to the white student's home; while "big shots" who appear to have been assigned to hall or cafeteria "duty" loudly warn anyone approaching the Negroes lunching alone to "stop that, if you don't want to get beaten up."

THIS SMALL, hard-core mob is easy to spot, both white and Negro students tell you in interviews outside the school, and several were suspended briefly for their cruelties. Most of them, sadly enough, are, in the vernacular, "lower-class whites" who come from marginal homes and neighborhoods and harbor general social grievances; the Negro is apparently a handy target for their hostilities.

At Ponders, a corner ice-cream, coke and sandwich shop opposite the school, you run into four youngsters of this group. They bear an astonishing resemblance to the tough-gang appearance of New York's problem children, a sort of Southern counterpart, down to their blue jeans, leather jackets, duck-tail haircuts, large-buckled belts and cigarettes.

"You can't print what I'd like to say about them jigs," one of them says in answer to a question.

"I have nothing to say to you," another said scornfully. "I'm a segregationist and you're from New York."

"Bates says she's going to get them out by September." He was referring to Mrs. Daisy Bates, president of the local branch of N. A. A. C. P. — the National Association for the Advancement of Colored People.

And one boy added; "We don't need knives like your kids use in New York. If I need to use anything, I use these." He shoved one foot up on the table; it wore a heavy leather cowboy-style boot.

Then the boy who had said he had nothing to say — a tall, handsome boy with a bitter face — stood up and said: "I'm a segregationist, but I'll be proud to show you this." He pulled from his wallet a printed identification card on which his name appeared as a member of the "N. A. A. C. P. — National Association for the Abolishment of Colored People."

HOW DO THE white students, the Negroes, the people of the community feel about this spectacle? You find out if you talk with them outside the school.

Some of the white students are uninterested in the plight of eight Negro pupils in a population of 2,000; either from indifference, or in self-defense, they ignore the Negroes, rather than risk being called "nigger lover" or being ostracized socially or worse. Some reflect the views of most respectable people here who do not belong to the extremist group but do not oppose it either, since emotionally they are in sympathy with its objectives ("They don't bother us because we don't talk to them." … "They've got their own schools, so why don't they stay there?" … "Well, they better not try to come to our dances.").

But there are others — no one can estimate how many — who would accept the Negroes but fear to make life more dangerous for them by avowing such friendships. For example, Ernest Green receives notes privately from white students who write that they "regret the situation" and tell him to keep his chin up.

AND ONE white student, who, in her own words, has become a "marked woman" since she befriended a Negro last year, is unafraid to speak up. Her mother, a newspaper woman, added briskly that she'd "disown the child if she hadn't shown some guts." She is Robin Wood, a 17-year-old beauty, whose fair hair, dimples, sparkle and outstanding scholarship have so far proved more than a match for her detractors.

"We were pretty calm about integration last summer," Robin said, "and I thought, 'Good old Little Rock, we'll be the leaders.' Then Faubus called out the troops and we were shocked. Then when Terrence came to English class, a boy and a girl walked out." Later, she loaned Terrence her algebra book and was promptly called "nigger lover" by someone who carefully explained to her that "anyone who's a nigger lover is either ignorant or a Communist."

One day she tore off the school bulletin board segregationist literature that had been smuggled onto it by the hard-core group, including a "Daisy Bates — WANTED" sign. Recently, she was told by a dancing partner, "You'd better not run for vice president of the Student Body because you're a moderate."

"I thought that the majority of the people were on my side," Robin went on. "But I think that the fence-straddling kids have gone over to the segregationists. If the moderates had spoken up for law and order and squelched the ones making the trouble, I think we would have won — but it looks like the other side is going to win. The majority of the whites won't come right out and be nice to the colored kids, because they've been scared."

MOST OF THE adult whites interviewed feared being identified in any way. Some literally looked over their shoulders in fear of being overheard, as though we were in East Berlin or Moscow. Some reflected their secret sympathy with the aims of the mob — to get the Negro students out of the school — but objected to their crude methods; others were outraged, but secretly, at the "black eye" given to Central High School and Little Rock generally, and expressed fears for the Negro students.

The attitudes of respectable white adults of the community are perhaps best verbalized in reports of two interviews.

One youthful mother, petite and gentle-voiced, waited in her car at school closing time for her son.

"You'll find that most of us don't like integration," she said, "and if there were anything we could do about it we probably would. But we don't approve of the shouting and violence. We feel that you can be a lady under any circumstances. And that if you can't change something gracefully, you should go along with it as best you can until another time presents itself. The quieter it can be, the better I like it. I wouldn't say that this experience has hurt my son. He hasn't let it bother him because he has nothing to do with them.

"Sometimes, I think the situation at Central is smoldering, because of bomb scares and the feeling inside."

ANOTHER SIDE of the picture came from a business man.

"I have no compunction at all about my children going to school with Negroes. They're human beings and are entitled to the same advantages as mine are. My wife and I profess to be Christians, and that's the motivating thing in our lives.

"But we're helpless. And I can sum up the reason in four words: I am a coward. Not for myself, but for my family. I don't want any crosses burning in my front yard. There are many who feel as I do, but we're disorganized, and afraid to express our opinions even to our best friends."

The Negro children — three boys and five girls — tell their own story, in deeds and in words.

SEVEN OF THEM were interviewed in Mrs. Daisy Bates' ranch house in an attractive residential part of town where Negro and white families lived peacefully for years, until last September. Since then a cross has burned on the Bates' front lawn, a bomb has blasted the lawn, their large front window remains taped together after a stoning, and their 12-year-old adopted son, Clyde, has been sent for safety to live with friends. (The eighth Negro student was too busy with homework to be present.)

As a group their morale is high. They reflect no psychological damage as a result of their ordeal, nor celebrity feelings because of the respect and admiration that the Negro community and their old Horace Mann classmates pay to them. They appear to be well aware of the pioneering role that they are playing.

They have been asked by school officials and Negro leaders not to retaliate against their tormentors, but to report incidents to the school authorities. But they tell you, with pride, that they do not report incidents, except when extreme — as, for example, when a white boy, after trying to shove a Negro girl downstairs, shouted: "I'll get you out of this school if I have to kill you."

THUS THEY DISLIKE talking about incidents. ("It's not so bad… "There's one kid who's always nice to me, but I can't tell you her name because she's already had trouble…" "No, I don't report the incidents any more; I can handle my problems…") But neither do they conceal their contempt for their torturers, or their concern for one another.

These eight, sole survivors of the original sixty-eight who applied for admission and became discouraged after the September outbreak, were screened well by their former principals for high scholarship, social stability and judgment They are, individually, as likable and interesting as any youngsters whose prime interests are getting a better education and making friends.

Elizabeth Eckford, a shy, reflective 16-year-old junior who wants to be a lawyer, said calmly that she had been spat on again that day, and that she now divides the students into three groups: "The majority who are civil-minded and courteous and who might like Negroes if they had a chance; those who antagonize verbally and not physically; and those who try to do physical harm to us. I knew it was going to be rough," she added, "but knowing it, and experiencing it, are different things."

Terrence, a proud, tall boy, was reticent about the extremists and voluble about "some kids who are friendly." He said most of the teachers are "real nice" and treat him "like an average student" (as when one dressed him down for reading a book of humorous poetry in his history class).

Gloria Ray, a bright-faced girl with a B-plus average, said, "I don't know very much about the whites. The only whites I come in contact with are those who are adverse to me. I feel just as isolated from the whites now as before I came to the school."

Would they do it again, knowing now what was in store? There were no quick answers. Elizabeth said she didn't know. Melba Patillo who had belonged "to every club we ever had" at Horace Mann, said, "It's hard to tell. We're not allowed to belong to anything here. They say the students aren't ready for us…" Terrence said, "Yes, because I'm getting a better education, and that's what I wanted." Gloria reflected, *I don't want to let my parents down…"

After the children had gone home, Mrs. Bates said: "We expect them to continue at Central High School next term — and we expect more to apply for entrance."

WHAT DOES this picture inside Central High School reveal today? It is that the situation is degenerating; that under the appearance of respectability, indifference to the explosive situation is being made a virtue; that so strong have the white extremists become in recent months that they have been able to stiffen up their psychological warfare not only against the decent white students but also against school officials.

In the early days, back at the beginning of the school year, this did not seem likely. The Federal Government had restored order. And for weeks after, the Capital City Citizens' Council segregationists were frightened and stopped their work. Now, with most of the troops gone, with cases against extremists thrown out of the local courts on a fines-paid basis, with the conviction that the Federal Government will not move against them, the segregationists are, as a civic leader put it, "riding high, wide and handsome."

Thus in recent weeks, the community witnessed the decision of the school board to reinstate the young segregationist they had expelled after officials had been harassed by bomb scares, news-paper ads, a court action and a television broadcast denouncing her expulsion.

Recently the police have been keeping close watch on the homes of the superintendent of schools, and the principal and vice principal of Central High School.

IN THE PRESENT ugly climate, there is fear that serious violence may be done to the Negro students if the guardsmen are removed from the school. It is an open secret that the extremists plan to stage a big-scale demonstration before graduation to prevent senior Ernest Green from marching with his class.

Some believe that the school officials might further retreat behind the "demonstrated fact that desegregation doesn't work" — and, clearly, it can hardly work under these conditions. Much depends on a pending court action on the Little Rock school board's petition to "postpone integration" — six months after the gradual integration plan has been in effect. The petition is opposed by the N. A. A. C. P.

There is also the strong possibility that Governor Faubus may ask for a special session of the Legislature, which could raise the emo-tional content again and result in more restrictive laws in advance of his coming campaign for re-election.

ONE THING is certain in the explosive situation. There is not likely to be any peace. Harry Ashmore, the executive editor of The Arkansas

Gazette, whose newspaper has been fighting for decency and moderation, sums up the situation this way:

"This is an intolerable situation. I don't know how it will be resolved. There is no local leadership to stand against the extremists. As long as they are backed by the full weight of the state government — which they are — there isn't much that the local people can do. The local people are cowed.

"They have no support from the city government, strong opposition from the state government, and no support from the Federal Government. What can the decent, law-abiding people do or hope to accomplish?

"Today, the small, militant bitter minority is in complete control. There is no real, widespread violence yet, but the potential is here. I suppose they'll take the kids one at a time."

The real crisis in Little Rock may just be beginning. And the crisis may be a reflection of the integration crisis all over the South.

GERTRUDE SAMUELS is a staff writer for The New York Times Sunday Magazine.

Little Rock Faces New School Fight

SPECIAL TO THE NEW YORK TIMES | MAY 31, 1958

LITTLE ROCK, ARK., MAY 30 — The only school at which Federal troops have been used to enforce a court's racial integration directive ended its first year of desegregated classes here this week.

The right of Negroes to attend the secondary institution, Central High School, is still being contested. A hearing will be held Tuesday in Federal District Court here on a school board request for permission to postpone implementation until 1961 of the board's plan for gradual desegregation of all the city's school system.

A 400-man federalized unit of the Arkansas National Guard has withdrawn from the school. However, President Eisenhower has indicated clearly that he would order troops back to the campus this fall if necessary to force compliance with court orders.

FIRST NEGRO GRADUATED

The school's first Negro graduate, Ernest Green, 16 years old, received his diploma on Tuesday night with 601 classmates. The ceremony took place without incident before an unsegregated audience of 4,000 persons.

The calm of the commencement exercise contrasted sharply with the rioting at Central High last September that followed the enrollment of Ernest and eight other Negroes.

Officials and community leaders were asked if the absence of trouble could be attributed to a "softening" of the general opposition to school desegregation in this capital. Many of them said that there had been no such change.

These persons credited the difference to a rallying of responsible elements here in opposition to a fairly small group of extremists and also to the firm stand taken by Little Rock's new police chief, Eugene Smith.

When a senior, Curtis E. Stover, 18, spat in the face of a Negro girl leaving baccalaurate exercises last Sunday night, Chief Smith arrested the youth promptly. Stover was charged with disorderly conduct and released in $200 bond for a hearing June 12.

ALL POLICE ON DUTY

All available policemen and detectives were called to duty on the night of the commencement exercises. Despite widespread rumors that white supremacists might try to cause trouble, not a murmur of dissent was heard from the audience as Ernest received his diploma.

Meanwhile, members of the League of Central High Mothers, a group bitterly opposed to integration, celebrated the end of eight months of surveillance by Federal troops at the school with a "Liberation Day" party.

For Ernest and two other boys and five girls who completed the term, the closing of school ended a period of tension and harassment at the hands of a small band of students favoring segregation.

A ninth Negro student, Minnijean Brown, 16, was suspended in February. She then enrolled in an integrated private school in New York.

Ernest said the students at Central High had not been "as bad as they've been pictured" in their treatment of the Negroes. "Many of them should be commended for the stand they took and the way in which they conducted themselves," he said.

AIMS TO BE LAWYER

Ernest has applied to Michigan State University for a scholarship. He would like to start this fall as pre-law student.

Although they pursued their studies under trying conditions in a new school with which they were unfamiliar, Ernest and the other seven Negro children earned average marks for the term. One of the Negroes, Carlotta Walls, 16, was on her class honor roll for the last six weeks.

The school board cited the troubled conditions that had existed at Central High in its petition for a delay in desegregating. It also remarked that the attitude of the community was "unfavorable" to the change.

The request for postponement is opposed by the National Association for the Advancement of Colored People. In a brief filed with the court the N. A. A. C. P. agreed that the school officials faced difficult problems. However, it said that board members had a constitutional duty "to follow through on their own plan approved by the court."

Little Rock Nine Awarded Medal

BY RUSSELL PORTER | **JULY 12, 1958**

CLEVELAND, JULY 11 — The Spingarn Medal for the highest achievement of an American Negro in 1957 was presented tonight to the nine Little Rock children and their adviser, Mrs. L. C. (Daisy) Bates.

The presentation was made by Dr. William E. Stevenson, president of Oberlin College, at the Forty-ninth annual convention of the National Association for the Advancement of Colored People.

The medal has been awarded annually since it was established in 1914 by the late J. E. Spingarn, chairman of the association's board of directors. His brother, Arthur B. Spingarn, is now president of the association.

Tonight's teen-age winners, six girls and three boys, were Minniejean Brown, Elizabeth Eckford, Ernest Green, Thelma Mothershed, Melba Pattillo, Gloria Ray, Terrence Roberts, Jefferson Thomas and Carlotta Walls.

They were honored for qualities shown in the face of threats and violence in attending the previously all-white Central High School in Little Rock, Ark., under the Supreme Court anti-segregation order. Mrs. Bates was honored for her leadership.

STUDENTS PRAISED FOR COURAGE

Dr. Stevenson said in a speech:

"We join in paying tribute to these ten great Americans. The Little Rock students have shown maturity, wisdom and courage, and have set an example for all people of goodwill everywhere to follow."

Ernest Green accepted on behalf of the nine. He said:

"We feel that Negroes, especially the younger generation, will not be satisfied until everyone is granted full democracy and until then America cannot take her place truly as world leader."

The citation that accompanied the award said it was made "in greater acknowledgment of their courageous self-restraint in the face of extreme provocation and peril and in recognition of their exemplary conduct in upholding American ideals of liberty and justice." It praised Mrs. Bates' inspiration, encouragement and guidance.

Mrs. Bates, who is the association's state president for Arkansas, accepted the medal "as a tribute to all the people of the South, Negro and white, who want our country to be in truth the land of the free."

APPEAL MADE TO EISENHOWER

Thurgood Marshall, director-counsel of the association's legal defense and educational fund, called on President Eisenhower for help to speed desegregation of public schools in the South.

In a speech at tonight's meeting, Mr. Marshall said:

"We must insist that the President declare publicly and unequivocally that he will not stand for another Little Rock.

"We must insist that the attorney General of the United States take forthright and vigorous action to prosecute any and all persons who openly violate the laws of the United States in regard to the Fourteenth Amendment and the Federal Civil Rights statutes.

"Without affirmative action by either the Executive or Legislative branch of the Federal Government we shall continue to resort to the courts for redress," he added. "We have no recourse but to continue our original plan to push forward with all deliberate speed."

Student From Little Rock

BY GERTRUDE SAMUELS | MAY 24, 1959

Minnijean Brown, who transferred to a New York high school, graduates next month.

ON FEB. 13, 1958, Minnijean Brown, a tall, proud, 16-year-old Negro girl, after being involved in a number of racial incidents in Central High School, Little Rock, Ark., retaliated to the taunts of a white girl who was calling her "nigger, nigger," with the retort, "white trash." She was expelled from the high school. "Minnijean had no right to retaliate," the principal said.

Then shocked and bewildered, Minnijean knew she could not return to the all-Negro Horace Mann High School from which she and eight other Negroes had transferred to Central High; that, she felt, would admit defeat of the integration experiment at Central High, and also encourage the segregationists there against her Negro classmates. Already cards were being circulated at the school reading, "One down, eight to go!" But she knew, too, that "I wanted an education — and that was the most important thing."

Now on June 5, Minnijean Brown will graduate with her classmates — from the New Lincoln High School in Manhattan. At the private, interracial school where she has been a scholarship student from the past fifteen months, her best friends include white and Negro students. She has been accepted by Michigan State University and also Upsala College in New Jersey. However, she has decided to enter Mt. Sinai Hospital School of Nursing in Manhattan, where she will begin three years of training to become a registered nurse. (Her mother is a practical nurse in Little Rock.)

"I know it sounds so idealistic," she tells you, "but lots of people need help, and I want to do whatever helps other people."

Ironically, as Minnijean finishes her high school education, all high schools in Little Rock remain closed. They have been closed the past school year, on order of the Governor, rather than continue with the desegregation program.

Though fifteen months here have not erased the Little Rock experience for Minnijean, they have given her a new perspective on the world outside Little Rock and on herself. This is the New York story of the girl whose name has become a symbol to her race and country.

SHE IS NOT a shy or reserved youngster. With her classmates at school, with the family with whom she has been living, dressing for a date or working at her studies, Minnijean participates enthusiastically in all activities. A large, handsome girl with shining black eyes, a quizzical smile or happy grin, she reflects the poise of a far older person in her ability to hide her feelings.

In the New Lincoln School, which has 431 students, of whom 15 per cent are Negroes, she had some critical adjustments to make when she arrived. First, she had to withstand the bombardment of publicity that follows pressures to be a "symbol." Reporters, photographers, television and radio people at first impressed, then frightened her as she worried about what her new friends would think of her.

Then, too, her previous educational background was a handicap in the rather advanced private school. She had inadequate training in science, mathematics and social studies, in the reading of good books and vocabulary building. Moreover, though endowed with "good, natural intellectual interests and adaptability," she did not bring with her an ability for consistent study; like many adolescents, Minnijean worked in the enthusiasm of the moment and found it difficult to follow through — on general work, reports, term papers.

THUS THE EARLY days of adjustment to school and her new home were difficult. On the human side, she had suffered from the jeers of Little Rock students and feared to look different from anyone else. She once called aside Mrs. Pauline Carpenter, who has since become one of her favorite teachers at New Lincoln:

"Are there any special socks or stockings worn here?" she asked, remembering Little Rock gibes. "What clothes must I wear?" Mrs. Carpenter replied that blouses and skirts were the usual daily dress, "and anything in which you feel comfortable."

Her way was further eased by the number of Negro and foreign exchange students who mingled freely in the school, and the realization that only her own dramatic experience made her stand out among them. Once in a while, someone would call her over to ask, "What really happened?" And for a few minutes, as a small group would gather, she would answer questions about Little Rock. But almost without noticing how it happened, she began to feel that she was in a normal school atmosphere and "just another student."

"What I wanted most," she recalls, "was to be accepted for myself — just as Minnijean Brown who transferred from another school."

Outstanding, say her teachers, are her adaptability and her compassion. Otherwise, Minnijean is an "average student" who must keep her nose to the grindstone. But you learn that her experience has also made her more understanding of people's behavior, in life and in literature, than youngsters of comparable or greater ability. Two examples illustrate this.

The first was a test of courage when, last year, her father shot and killed a man in Little Rock. He was convicted of manslaughter after pleading self-defense and sentenced to five years' imprisonment. (An appeal is pending.) The girl suffered quietly during her father's trial and "wanted to collapse or escape," but instead went on with her life here as her mother and her new friends expected her to do.

The second example occurred when the seniors were discussing possible speakers for a program. Minnijean suggested that one topic might be the Southern liberals' position in areas where desegregation is taking place. "I don't think people appreciate how difficult it has been for some of the liberals in Arkansas," she told her classmates, "and many of them have been very good to me."

The New Lincoln School experience has given Minnijean a truer measure of the world outside Little Rock and, she feels, helped her to "grow up here."

"I think that segregation is a burden that pushes people of both races down," she tells you, "because it makes young Negroes feel inferior, while it makes the whites feel they have the right to feel superior, which isn't so. And because of these feelings it brings a lot of silly hatred on both sides."

"INTEGRATION CAN WORK because now I've seen it work at this school, and this proves it. From what happened in Little Rock, I didn't know what to expect when I came here, because I'd never seen integration work peacefully this way. Here my friends of both races are just friends. 'We agree sometimes and we disagree sometimes, and color is not important."

One is impressed with the intrinsic poise of the girl, but perhaps the most important influence on her life here has been the Clark family with whom she came to live.

Drs. Mamie and Kenneth Clark are Negro psychologists — she heads the Northside Center For Child Development, a rehabilitation center for underprivileged children; he is an Associate Professor of Psychology at City College and also serves on the New York State Youth Commission. They have a teenage son and daughter, and in their informal, riverside home at Pinecrest, an interracial district of Hastings-on-the-Hudson, Minnijean felt that she was a member of the family. She shared a room with the daughter Kate, now a freshman at Oberlin, and stayed on after Kate left for college last September and the son Hilton entered Kent School in Connecticut.

For the Clarks, Minnijean brought a spontaneous joy with her, often singing popular music and blues at the top of her voice as she did chores with Kate. Evenings, she helped to support herself with baby-sitting in Hastings. The girls, with typical adolescent fervor, soon "adored" each other, shared secrets and clothes and, Mrs. Clark ruefully observes, had the same sloppy habits about their room.

IT WAS THE Clarks who made Minnijean feel it was important not to let the past dominate her future, to put it in perspective and not let it become a burden. Conversely, one of their hardest jobs was to keep people from exploiting the youngster who was flattered at first by requests for appearances and speeches.

Dr. Mamie Clark, tiny, feminine and firm, said no to all requests. She explained to Minnijean that she was here to study, that she had to prepare herself for the future, and not in terms of Little Rock or of people trying to exploit her identification with Little Rock. At times, Minnijean seemed susceptible to the flattery, even hostile to suggestions that she resist it.

The lionizing once led her to think that she would be "discovered" and have a singing career. In this case. Mamie Clark quietly let her have her way. Minnijean entered a Peekskill talent show, singing "I've Got the Whole World in My Hands," only to discover that Hollywood scouts really wouldn't be in the audience as her fantasy had led her to think, and that her voice was somewhat less than professional. Afterward, she calmly said she had been silly as Mamie Clark again brought her back to realities.

It is the love, understanding and example that Minnijean was able to accept from the Clarks that she cherishes above all. "They took me in as one of the family and gave me advice and understanding. They are my pattern," she tells you, "and I will never forget this."

The other day, as she prepared to study in her red-and-white bedroom strewn with records, books on economics, modern physics and French, and with the radio playing "I Feel Pretty" from "West Side Story" ("I can't study without the radio going"), Minnijean summed up this phase of her life:

"Watching myself awaken to the new way of things here — watching myself really grow up here," she said, "and to be able to analyze so many things that happened to me in Little Rock and here — these are the biggest impressions of the past year or so. The New York experience opened a complete new world for me.

"Maybe I would have found this at home. But being able to see good people who aren't prejudiced, who believe in the same things that I believe in — I mean white people as well as Negroes, because I never saw that at home — has renewed my faith in everything.

"Because when I was home I thought, is it worth it? It was like running into a brick wall. But now I know that there are many young people who want to do something very constructive for other young people.

"BUT THERE IS just one problem," she went on slowly, "Some people are sort of unfair to me — they expect more of me than I am. They seem to think I should be a sophisticated leader, and I'm not. There are all kinds of things that go into being a leader, and a leader isn't just having a name that people can applaud. It needs special qualifications and training and education. I think that in time I could be a leader, and I want to be one. But most people don't become prominent until they become a little older. People should remember that."

And the wise old child of 17 turned up the radio a bit more as she turned back to her homework for tomorrow.

GERTRUDE SAMUELS of The New York Times Magazine won an American Newspaper Guild Page One Award for her stories from Little Rock.

CHAPTER 2

Freedom Riders

The Freedom Riders organized groups, planned routes
and rode interstate buses throughout the South, testing
segregation laws and highlighting the Southern states'
failure to comply with the 1956 Supreme Court decision to
desegregate public buses. Mobs of angry white protesters
verbally and physically abused the riders in multiple cities.
In spite of these attacks, the riders remained unwavering
in their resolve. Their bravery forced lawmakers to confront
the unresolved bus and terminal segregation, eventually
ensuring that the law was upheld.

2 'Freedom' Buses Linked by Youth

BY RICHARD P. HUNT | MAY 22, 1961

A NEGRO DIVINITY STUDENT in Nashville, Tenn., was the direct link
between the original "Freedom Riders" and those now at the center of
the Alabama race dispute.

He was identified yesterday as John Lewis of Troy, Ala., a student
at the American Baptist Theological Institute, who left the original
"Freedom Ride" and returned to Nashville to take an examination.

In a telephone interview, the Rev. James M. Lawson Jr., organizer
of the Nashville Nonviolent Movement, said in Nashville yesterday
that Mr. Lewis had planned to rejoin the original "Freedom Ride" at
Montgomery, Ala., after his examination.

As Mr. Lawson explained it, events then took this course:

The original Freedom Riders, a group then composed of thirteen men and women, six whites and seven Negroes who belonged to the Congress of Racial Equality — were beaten by whites a week ago yesterday at Anniston, Ala., and Birmingham, Ala.

This group had left Washington on May 5, intending to travel by bus to New Orleans in a challenge to segregation in the vehicles, restaurants and waiting rooms of bus companies.

By 6 o'clock last Monday morning members of the Nashville Nonviolent Movement, with which Mr. Lewis is affiliated, decided to support the Freedom Ride project. Early Tuesday, some were on the way to Alabama.

In the meantime, the Congress of Racial Equality group had abandoned the freedom ride, and the original riders had returned to their homes. Last Wednesday members of the Nashville group arrived in Birmingham and attempted to carry on.

On that day seven members of the Nashville group tried, and failed, to ride a bus to Montgomery from Birmingham. The police took them into "protective custody" until Friday morning, when they were driven to the Tennessee state line.

The students returned to Birmingham by car. In the meantime, twelve more students from Nashville had arrived to reinforce them. On Saturday the group went on to Montgomery by bus, and were attacked by crowds of whites when they arrived.

"Efforts are now under way to enlarge the project into a South-wide movement involving the whole nonviolent movement," Mr. Lawson said.

The Nashville Nonviolent Movement group of Freedom Riders started with three whites, one each from Tennessee, Wisconsin and California, and sixteen Negroes.

WON SIT-IN CAMPAIGN

Their movement has won several successes in anti-segregation campaigns within the last fifteen months. Last year their "sit-ins" forced integration of cafeterias in Nashville 10-cent stores. This year downtown motion picture houses in Nashville were integrated.

The Nashville Nonviolent Movement is an action group formed by the Nashville Christian Leadership Council and the Student Central Committee, a body of delegates from student organizations on college campuses in and around Nashville.

The Nashville Christian Leadership Council is an affiliate of the Southern Christian Leadership Council of which the Rev. Dr. Martin Luther King Jr. is president. Mr. Lawson is a vice president of the Nashville Christian Leadership Council.

The colleges represented in the Student Central Committee are Fisk University, the American Baptist Theological Seminary, Tennessee Agricultural and Industrial State University, George Peabody College, Vanderbilt University Medical School and Meharry Medical College.

Montgomery Tension High After Threats of Bombing

BY CLAUDE SITTON | MAY 23, 1961

MONTGOMERY, ALA., TUESDAY, MAY 23 — National Guardsmen are enforcing an uneasy truce here under martial law following renewed racial violence. Bomb threats, two attempted house-burnings and minor incidents kept tension high in this first capital of the Old Confederacy in the wake of efforts to end segregation on interstate buses and in waiting rooms.

Some 1,800 pupils were evacuated from two junior high schools after telephoned bomb threats. Similar threats were received at the Greyhound bus station and Radio Station WAPX.

The police and firemen found no explosives.

Flaming "Molotov cocktails," bottles of gasoline stoppered with rags, were tossed at two homes yesterday but neither was damaged. One house was occupied by Negroes and the other by a white restaurant operator who was acquitted recently in the shotgun slaying of a member of the Ku Klux Klan.

White-helmeted troops in green fatigues rolled through the streets in jeeps. Others with slung rifles stood watch at bus, train and airport terminals.

One hundred additional National Guardsmen were called to the Greyhound Bus Terminal late last night. It was feared there might be trouble, with several buses scheduled to arrive close together. There was no incident, and the men were ordered to return to their posts.

A spokesman at the terminal reported that business was being conducted as usual.

Some 550 deputy Federal marshals were held in readiness at Maxwell Air Force Base within the city. Two hundred more were rushing here on orders from Robert F. Kennedy, the Attorney General.

The local police and the state highway patrol were also on the alert. Concern was expressed over reports that Negro and white "Freedom Riders" would renew their efforts to carry the anti-segregation drive on across Alabama and into Mississippi and Louisiana.

Judge Walter B. Jones has ordered the demonstrators to show cause today in Montgomery's Circuit Court why they should not be found in contempt. He had earlier issued an injunction against them forbidding a continuation of their activities.

Some observers said this might lead to a showdown between state and Federal authorities. The Justice Department has said that it would protect the rights of bus passengers.

State officials have contended that the demonstrators violated Alabama's segregation laws. Whites and Negroes among them have shared seats on buses and have sought service in terminal restaurants restricted to either white or Negro passengers.

The Supreme Court has ruled that a state cannot enforce segregation in transportation. This is so whether bus, plane or train is used or whether the journey crosses a state border. The court has also found that interstate waiting rooms in terminals may not be segregated. In a ruling this term, it decided also that a private restaurant in an interstate terminal designed to serve interstate passengers could not be segregated.

Gov. John Patterson, who imposed martial law here last night, is expected to address a joint session of the Legislature at noon today on the controversy.

In a statement yesterday, he reiterated his contention that "the Federal Government has no business or legal authority to interfere in our internal problems."

He continued:

"I am saddened by the recent incidents in Alabama calculatedly provoked by a group of irresponsible outsiders. I say again that Alabama will enforce the law diligently and fearlessly. State authorities together with the Alabama National Guard are fully able and will control the local situation."

The statement came in response to telegrams from some other Southern governors endorsing his position.

A BUS WAS BURNED

The demonstration on wheels began in Washington under the sponsorship of the Congress of Racial Equality. Angry whites attacked one group last week in Anniston, Ala., and then put the torch to a bus on which another group was riding.

When the riders reached Birmingham, a bloody riot ensued. The demonstrators discontinued their efforts and left the state by plane.

But other demonstrators from the Nashville, Tenn., Student Nonviolent Committee boarded a bus in Birmingham last Saturday and reached Montgomery.

A second riot broke out here upon their arrival and a third came Sunday when they gathered at a Negro mass meeting in the First Baptist Church.

PAUL SCHUTZER/THE LIFE PICTURE COLLECTION/GETTY IMAGES

National Guardsmen helping Freedom Riders back to their homes after an angry mob besieged a church rally earlier this month.

Federal marshals, and, later, the city police and highway patrolmen, held a mob of whites at bay with tear gas and night sticks. An automobile was overturned and burned and a number of persons were injured.

The 1,500 Negroes at the mass meeting spent the night in the church at the request of officials. At one point tear gas filtered into the church and caused a slight panic. As dawn arrived, the guardsmen began escorting the participants home in small groups, while mobile units patrolled the area.

James Farmer, national director of the Congress of Racial Equality, said Monday that five Freedom Riders would make an attempt to resume the demonstration here, probably today.

Meantime, James Bevel, chairman of the Nashville group and a student at the American Baptist Theological Seminary there, said in Nashville that the group there also planned to go ahead with the drive.

The Rev. Dr. Martin Luther King Jr. of Atlanta, president of the Southern Christian Leadership Conference, and other Negro leaders met here late yesterday to plan other anti-segregation activities.

Meanwhile, interstate buses entering the state were stopped for Alabama highway patrolmen to read the state court order barring more persons seeking to end segregation. Officials said this was done to put riders "on notice" so that violators of the injunction could receive contempt citations.

Byron R. White, Deputy Attorney General and the top Justice Department official on the scene, discounted last night the likelihood of any conflict between states forces and the deputy marshals. He emphasized that the marshals had been brought in only to preserve order.

Mr. White said that if the marshals were needed again they would be brought in after consultation with Maj. Gen. Henry V. Graham, the state adjutant general. The two conferred this morning.

"We told him we were available to protect Federal rights here," said the Deputy Attorney General. "He indicated there might be occasions on which we could help and we indicated that we were ready to do so. We will remain here for a few days not only in the event of disturbances in Montgomery but wherever they might develop."

Mr. White conceded that the department had no solution to the problem posed by the Freedom Riders. "We think they have a right to travel freely and safely in interstate commerce," he said.

After comment on the threat to the bi-racial group posed by Judge Jones action, he pointed out that they could file a court test of any penalties imposed on them.

He also said the Justice Department was investigating the violent outbreaks here, in Birmingham and in Anniston. He said arrests would be made if evidence of Federal violations was found.

In another news conference, the deputy in charge of the marshals at the riot last night said they had moved in only after a state investigator had requested them to do so. The deputy is William D. Behen, the assistant supervisor of the Federal Alcohol and Tobacco Tax Unit in Florida.

The force of marshals is under the command of James P. McShane, United States Marshal for the District of Columbia.

The Chamber of Commerce unanimously adopted a resolution calling on President Kennedy to "recall and remove the Federal marshals and other law enforcement officers from the City of Montgomery forthwith and without delay."

Chamber members said they "abhorred" violence but that the continued presence of the deputy marshals "may well provoke further breaches of the peace." They also said "the situation is well in hand at this time."

The force of marshals here is under James P. McShane, the United States Marshal for the District of Columbia.

The Montgomery Advertiser criticized Governor Patterson for his role in the controversy. In an editorial for tomorrow's edition, Grover C. Hall Jr., editor, declared:

Patterson is not the exclusive author of Montgomery's troubles by any means, but his is the supreme responsibility as chief guardian against disorder.

The measure of the errors is this. These 'Freedom Rider' incendiaries passed through every state from Washington to Alabama. But only Alabama among these states now has a problem because of it.

This kind of jungle life could make Montgomery a depressed area. The Lord alone knows what the derelictions in law enforcement have and will cost Montgomery economically.

There is naught to do but recognize the damage and the intolerable condition that exist and set ourselves to trudging the road back.

There is only one road. The people have got to understand that leaving matters to mobs is calamity. The people have got to demand that their officials collar and jail mobsters as routinely as they give parking tickets.

Negro Girl a Force in Campaign; Encouraged Bus to Keep Rolling

BY DAVID HALBERSTAM | MAY 23, 1961

WASHINGTON, MAY 22 — The driving force behind the Nashville student protest group is a spirited Negro girl from Chicago.

As Negro leaders were meeting today in Montgomery, Ala., to decide on their next steps, Diane Nash, 22 years old, told a reporter over the phone from that city:

"We will not stop. There is only one outcome."

Miss Nash left Fisk University in Nashville this year as a senior to give more time to segregation protests. She is working full time as coordinating secretary of the Nashville Nonviolent Movement. This is the student group that led successful protests against lunch-counter and movie-theatre segregation.

Early last week, when the first "freedom riders" decided to cut short their protest tour at Birmingham, Ala., the Nashville group unanimously decided to complete the itinerary.

SAW THEIR CHANCE

"We saw this as a chance to go ahead, and the kids wanted to go," Miss Nash said. "All the kids knew that death was a real possibility on this trip. John Lewis [a student who had made the first part of the trip] told us how rough it was. Each kid who went on the bus said he was willing to give his life."

Miss Nash is credited with the determination that has kept the protest movement alive more than a year after its victory at the lunch counters.

As she organized the bus protest last week, a Justice Department official talked with her in Nashville and attempted to have her delay the trip.

He said he sympathized with her objectives but believed that to make the trip at this time, with feeling so high in Alabama, would be dangerous and irresponsible.

"It was as if I were talking to a wall," the official said later. "She never listened to a word."

"We aren't going to stop, not now," she declared, "Why, those people in Alabama think they can ignore the President of the United States, and they think they can still win by beating us Negroes over the head."

Miss Nash kept the Nashville group at work last summer by devoting her vacation to studying the potential of nonviolence in demolishing segregation barriers.

She has been in jail twice as a result of the lunch-counter movement. The first time, in Nashville last spring, was for one day. Earlier this year she was jailed for thirty days at Rock Hill, S. C.

During the bus protest, Miss Nash did not actually ride in a bus. She was used as an "executive officer," a decision made by her fellow demonstrators, who feared she might be jailed again or beaten. But she joined the present group in Montgomery.

Most members of her group are students at Fisk, Tennessee State University and American Baptist Seminary, all Negro schools. They are mostly from middle-class homes, dress in Ivy style and are concerned with the relationship of Christianity to their social protests.

Advising these youths in Nashville and throughout the South are young Negro Protestant ministers, many of whom have been educated in Northern universities.

Several times in the struggle, as in the bus protest, the movement has acted spontaneously without direction from the ministers.

It became so successful, or so deeply committed, that it was endorsed by the ministers and organization led by the Rev. Dr. Martin Luther King, known as the Southern Christian Leadership Council.

Last Saturday, Dr. King and his colleagues from other Southern cities quickly gathered with the youths in Montgomery to work jointly on their next step.

This means decisions on how big to make the bus protest, whether to go to Mississippi and whether to launch parallel bus assaults on segregation laws in several states at the same time.

In Nashville, the movement had dwindled since the early days of the sit-ins, when it was campus-wide. The more casual students had returned to their normal ways of studying, dating and staying out of jail. But according to Miss Nash, the beating of their classmates and the opening of a new avenue of protest "has given us more strength."

"They beat us," she said, "and we're stronger than ever."

27 Bi-Racial Bus Riders Jailed in Jackson, Miss., as They Widen Campaign

BY CLAUDE SITTON | MAY 25, 1961

JACKSON, MISS., MAY 24 — Twenty-seven "Freedom Riders" were arrested and jailed today after coming here from Montgomery. Ala., in buses under armed military escort.

No violence resulted from the attempts of the two groups to challenge segregation in bus terminals, despite rising racial tension that produced a series of riots in Alabama in the last ten days.

Mississippi National Guard officers reported that a threat had been made to dynamite the first bus as it crossed the state line. The threat was not carried out.

SERVED AT LUNCH COUNTER

Some of the twenty-five Negroes and two white persons in the two groups made successful demands for service at the lunch counter in the white waiting room of the Trailways Bus Terminal in Montgomery before leaving there.

However, four of the first group were arrested when they sought to enter white rest rooms in the station here after their arrival at 3:55 P. M. Eastern daylight time. The eight others were seized inside the white men's rest room a few minutes later.

The bus carrying the other demonstrators pulled into the terminal at 6:47 P. M. Three minutes later, all fifteen had been arrested. They had lined up in front of the entrance to the terminal's white cafeteria and had refused the demand from Police Capt. J. L. Ray that they leave.

All were charged with breach of the peace in refusing to obey an officer. They were held in lieu of bonds totaling $1,000 each of the two charges. Before leaving the Alabama capital, their leaders had vowed that the demonstrators would remain in jail rather than post bond or pay a fine.

Jack Travis, the city Prosecutor, said that they would probably be tried Friday. They face a maximum penalty of fines amounting to $700 and ten months imprisonment.

RIOT CHARGES DROPPED

The first twelve arrested were also charged with inciting to riot but this charge was dropped later.

The Supreme Court has ruled that a state cannot enforce segregation in any form of transportation. The court has also found that interstate waiting rooms in terminals may not be segregated. In a ruling this term, it decided also that a private restaurant in an interstate terminal designed to serve interstate passengers could not be segregated.

Among those arrested was James Farmer, national director of the Congress of Racial Equality of New York. C. O. R. E., as the organization is popularly known, started the Freedom Ride the first week of May in Washington.

The original destination was New Orleans. However, the C. O. R. E. demonstrators, most of whom were non-Southerners, returned to their homes after a bus was burned in Anniston, Ala., and they had been attacked there and again in Birmingham.

SEEN OFF BY DR. KING

Other demonstrators, members of Nashville's Student Nonviolent Committee, resumed the campaign last Wednesday and finally boarded a bus for Montgomery Saturday.

The Rev. Dr. Martin Luther King Jr., principal leader of the "nonviolent action" espoused by the students, saw them off in Montgomery this morning. He said he expected that there would be Freedom Riders on many of the buses leaving Montgomery within the next few weeks.

The buses carried no general riders — only the Freedom Riders, about twenty newsmen and some Guardsmen, who rode part of the time with bayonets fixed.

The big Vista View red and white Trailways buses that carried the demonstrators halfway across Alabama and into Mississippi passed up all stations on the way. This led to a controversy on the first bus. One of the demonstrators accused Lieut. Col. Gillespie V. Montgomery of "degrading and inhumane" treatment in refusing to halt for a rest stop.

The first party pulled out of the Montgomery terminal at 9:12 A.M. After the escort of National Guardsmen and highway patrolmen was changed at the state line, the Rev. C. T. Vivian, 36 years old, of the Cosmopolitan Community Church of Nashville, Tenn., approached the Mississippi officer and made his request to stop. The colonel said that he did not have authority to stop the bus.

"This is degrading us," the minister asserted after the National Guardsman ordered him to return to his seat.

REFUSED SECOND TIME

Mr. Vivian returned to speak with Colonel Montgomery twenty-five minutes later and said it was imperative that he and others among the Freedom Riders be allowed to make a rest stop. He was again refused permission.

The route taken by the buses — United States Route 80 — leads through the heart of the Black Belt, an area of dark soil and a large Negro population. Militant segregationists hold the reigns of power throughout much of this strip and race relations have made relatively little progress.

Jackson is the modern capital of segregation, the home base of the Citizens' Council movement, which wields strong influence in state governmental affairs.

Mississippi's Governor, Ross R. Barnett, campaigned on a platform of unrelenting opposition to desegregation and pledged to go to jail if necessary to prevent its coming.

Nevertheless, the councils, Mr. Barnett and leading citizens urged that there be no repetition here of the violence that broke out in Alabama. A front-page editorial today in The State Times probably represented the sentiments of many Mississippians.

The newspaper's editor, Oliver Emmerich, said that the Freedom Riders had failed in Georgia, Virginia, North and South Carolina because they did not "obtain their objective to stir up violence." He continued:

"When the 'Freedom Riders' reach Mississippi we do not want them to have their efforts crowned with success. Their objective is to make the headlines. They want to stir up violence. The more violent the people, the more successful their campaign. Theirs is a grandstand play, and we should receive it as such.

"...We must recognize this is a test for Mississippi. We urge our people to show restraint in the face of these unwanted visitors who seek to besmirch Mississippi's good name."

Dr. King held a brief prayer meeting for the Freedom Riders in Montgomery before they were escorted to the bus station by National Guardsmen. When they arrived, the street on which the terminal is located had been blocked off by 250 soldiers with bayonets fixed and rifles held high.

Maj. Gen. Henry V. Graham, the State Adjutant General, took personal command of the operation. He said that 1,000 Guardsmen had already taken up positions along the route to the Mississippi line. Floyd Mann, the State Commissioner of Public Safety, also was on hand.

RIDE NOT 'A VALID TEST'

Before the bus pulled out, Dr. King told newsmen that the Freedom Riders would not consider this ride "a valid test" of bus desegregation and expressed hope that one day such precautions would not be necessary.

General Graham boarded the bus and warned the one white and eleven Negro demonstrators and some twenty newsmen that "this could be a hazardous trip." He noted that Gov. John Patterson had ordered him and Mr. Mann to prevent any trouble and he said that none was expected.

"We wish you — sincerely — a good trip," he said, smiling, and left the bus to take his position in the command car.

Forty-one vehicles, including sixteen highway patrol cruisers each carrying three combat-equipped National Guardsmen and two troopers, accompanied the bus.

A squad of city motorcycle policemen headed the column to the city limits, where the patrol cruisers took over with their red dome lights flashing.

As Fred Stokes, the 25-year-old driver, drove the bus over the bridge across the Alabama River, the riders sang a sit-in song to the Calypso tune of "Day O."

Freedom, give us freedom,
Freedom's coming and it won't be long.

Three L-19 reconnaissance planes and two helicopters circled overhead.

A farmer following a motorized cultivator raised one hand as the bus passed and thumbed his nose.

As the convoy passed through Selma at 10:33 A.M., a roughly dressed group of whites shouted curses and threats.

At the rear of the bus, the Rev. James M. Lawson, pastor of the Scott Chapel Methodist Church of Shelbyville, Tenn., and one of Dr. King's leading disciples, conducted a workshop on "nonviolent action."

"If we get knocked down too often, let's kneel together where we are," he told the eleven others at one point.

The convoy made several stops at isolated spots along the highway.

Sixty miles from the Mississippi line the bus passed through another community, most of whose populace turned out to see the show. A white man stuck out his tongue at the passing bus and a Negro woman across the street smiled and waved, her fingers reaching out as if to touch the vehicle.

At Demopolis, Ala., another white man shook his fist and a hard object struck the side of the bus. Others in the crowd along the highway jeered and shouted curses.

The Alabamans turned the bus over to a much smaller escort of Mississippi National Guardsmen and highway patrolmen at 2:10 P.M. The Mississippians were under the command of Maj. Gen. W. P. Wilson.

The city police here had cleared the Trailways Terminal of spectators and had stationed fifty men inside and outside. Three German shepherd police dogs imported from Vicksburg were held on leashes in front of the station.

Group Maps Plans on Freedom Rides

BY CLAUDE SITTON | JUNE 1, 1961

ATLANTA, MAY 31 — The telephone rang constantly in Room 103 of the modernistic building of old brick, new glass and wood paneling at 197 ½ Auburn Avenue.

Students called in to volunteer for a test of segregation in transportation terminals across the South. Plans were discussed. News from demonstrators in Montgomery, Ala., and Jackson, Miss., was relayed to other cities in the South and North.

Young Negroes in sport shirts, Ivy League suits and print dresses talked over strategy amid a clutter of filing cabinets, tables piled high with newspapers and pamphlets, chairs and a lone desk. Two installers squeezed in to ask about a request for an additional telephone.

This windowless, second-floor cubicle houses the nerve center for the latest assault on Southern segregation, the command post of the Freedom Ride Coordinating Committee.

FORMED BY FOUR GROUPS

The committee was formed last Friday at a conference here of representatives from four integration organizations. They are the Southern Christian Leadership Conference, the Student Nonviolent Coordinating Committee, the Nashville (Tenn.) Christian Leadership Council and the Congress of Racial Equality.

One of those on the committee is Edward B. King Jr., 21 years old, the administrative secretary of the Student Nonviolent Coordinating Committee, which was set up a year ago by Southern students participating in lunch-counter sit-ins.

Mr. King, who will serve as recruiting chief for the Freedom Rides, toyed with a blue-on-white button that said, "I believe in human dignity.

"Even at the risk of losing public favor, we are willing to go on," he said. "I hope the public will keep in mind that this is a moral issue. The enthusiasm has been tremendous."

PEAK ACTIVITY LOOMS

He said that the peak of activity would likely be reached next week, when many students leave college for the summer. The committee already has promises of volunteer groups of riders, from Wesleyan, Yale and Duke Universities, he said. Duke is an all-white institution in Durham, N. C.

Mr. King emphasized that the Freedom Riders would reject persons unwilling to go to jail and stay there. Those who post bond or pay fines "damage the morale" of the ones who refuse to do so, he said.

He and his assistant, Rodney Powell, 25, who will be graduated from Meharry Medical School at Nashville this year, would not rule out the likelihood of further violence. "It's not necessary but it's probably inevitable that someone will be hurt," Mr. Powell said.

One of the top adults in the new committee is the Rev. Wyatt T. Walker, executive director of the Southern Christian Leadership Conference.

The minister said that the students would probably handle most of the work of the committee, although he would serve as an adviser. He conceded that there "is a lot of cloak and dagger as far as the student posture is concerned." But he said, "They are the ones serving as the shock troops and we've got to go along."

How Jim Crow Travels in South

BY CLAUDE SITTON | JUNE 4, 1961

MONTGOMERY, ALABAMA, JUNE 3 — The Negro faces a jungle of law and custom in Southern transportation despite Federal attempts to end segregation. Practices vary so widely throughout the region that uncertainty often leads him to surrender to tradition even where racial barriers are non-existent.

Aroused by the "freedom rides" and their sometimes violent aftermath, Attorney General Robert F. Kennedy acted this week to deal with an important facet of the problem. He asked the Interstate Commerce Commission to adopt stringent regulations against segregation in interstate bus terminals.

It is difficult to predict at this point how effective the Justice Department's implementation can be if the request is granted. Similar efforts in this general field have bogged down in the past because of legal problems and a lack of adequate enforcement.

The progress, the lack of progress and the confusion is apparent to any Negro who travels from Atlanta to Montgomery, for example. He could catch a desegregated trolley to a desegregated Greyhound terminal in the Georgia capital and board a desegregated bus. But when the bus made a rest stop at La Grange, Ga., he would find separate waiting rooms marked "White" and "Colored."

AT MONTGOMERY

Upon arriving in Montgomery, he again would be faced with two waiting rooms, one occupied solely by Negroes and the other by whites. But he would see no signs restricting them to either race. And no one could tell him with certainty what would happen if he entered the "White" waiting room and ordered coffee.

If the passenger chose to come by train he might encounter difficulty in the station restaurant in Atlanta. Negro sit-in demonstrators have been arrested there on charges of violating Georgia's anti-trespass law. Conversely, he might be given the same treatment accorded whites.

Although he would be an interstate traveler, he would have to decide after reaching Montgomery whether to enter the "Colored intrastate waiting room" or the "White intrastate waiting room." The Union Station here has no "interstate" facilities. This oversight is common to most bus and rail terminals in the South and is a seemingly deliberate one designed to evade I. C. C. regulations.

The restrictive signs on the entrances carry the notation, "By order of the Alabama Public Service Commission." But officials of that agency readily concede that state segregation laws may be invalid in view of a 1956 Supreme Court decision outlawing the practice on this city's buses.

If the hypothetical traveler decided to ride a plane, he would be struck by the even greater contrast. He would be free to sit where he chose, eat where he chose and drink where he chose in Atlanta's new air terminal. He might even share a seat with a white passenger enroute. But the barrier of segregation would slam down between them once they stepped off the plane.

EVEN WATER FOUNTAINS

Illuminated signs designate the "Negro" and "White" waiting rooms and rest rooms at Montgomery's Danelly Field, which was built in 1958 with Federal assistance. Even the water fountains standing side by side in the ticket counter lobby are marked "White Only" and "Colored Only." The steps beside them are placed at opposite ends of the fountains as if to prevent children of the two races from brushing against each other.

In interstate travel, such practices are generally confined to terminals. Few attempts are made to enforce segregation on buses and trains themselves. Planes have never been affected.

Restrictions are still found on many bus lines and a few railroads operating within the borders of a given state. However, they are being eased as the result of voluntary action, economic pressure and Federal court orders.

In the matter of custom, many Negroes continue to sit in the rear of buses. Cases of their sharing seats with whites are rare. Leaders in the desegregation struggle have complained frequently over this failure to exercise newly-won rights.

Forced segregation on interstate or intrastate carriers violates Federal law as interpreted on numerous occasions by the Supreme Court. Following the Court's 1954 school desegregation ruling, the I. C. C. banned segregation in an interstate rail terminal. This was later upheld by the Supreme Court.

The justices went a step further in a ruling last December involving a Trailways bus terminal restaurant in Richmond, Va. They held that although the facility was not operated by the bus line itself, the proprietor must end segregation since he was dependent upon bus passengers for patronage.

In extending these actions to the South as a whole, Mr. Kennedy faces the same basic legal barrier that is retarding school desegregation. This is a fact that Supreme Court decisions, as well as most I. C. C. rulings, set precedents but do not generally force compliance by states and communities not involved in the case at hand.

The proof of this lies in the continued segregation of some southern rail terminals despite I. C. C. policy backed up by the Supreme Court. A Federal court order has been obtained only recently to end racial restrictions in Birmingham, Ala. And a group of freedom riders was arrested last week in Jackson, Miss., while using "White" terminal facilities in that city's railroad station.

Even if the commission's rulings applied to all rail and bus carriers, the agency still would be hampered in policing them because of a small staff.

As a result, the surest way to force desegregation now is through private court suits, a long and tedious process if the entire South is to be brought into line.

If the commission grants Mr. Kennedy's request, the bus lines will be prohibited in effect from using any segregated terminal, including those operated by private individuals. The latter are the strongholds of segregation. Since they are not engaged, as are the carriers, in interstate commerce, they are not under the commission's jurisdiction.

AIRPORT QUESTION

There is no ready solution to the problem presented by segregation in airline terminals. Although Federal funds have been used in their construction, this assistance was restricted during the Eisenhower administration to "non-segregated areas" of the structures. Federal officials doubt whether they have jurisdiction because of this.

Furthermore, the Civil Aeronautics Board has taken a different approach from that of the I. C. C. Its policy is that the terminals are not integral parts of the airline system and therefore not subject to its regulatory powers.

President Supports Travel Right of All

BY TOM WICKER | JULY 20, 1961

WASHINGTON, JULY 19 — President Kennedy upheld today the right of American citizens to move in interstate commerce "for whatever reasons they travel."

The President stopped short of an endorsement of the Freedom Riders movement, about which he was asked to comment at his news conference.

"The basic question," he said, "is not the Freedom Riders. The basic question is that anyone who moves in interstate commerce should be able to do so freely."

Some Southerners have said that the Freedom Riders deliberately sought to arouse the kind of violence that followed their arrival in Birmingham and Montgomery, Ala., in May. The Government should stop persons traveling for such purposes, they contended.

Senator John Stennis, Mississippi Democrat, introduced legislation to that effect.

Mr. Kennedy, in effect, rejected this argument, although he stipulated that the constitutional right to travel should be "exercised in a peaceful way."

"Whether we agree with those who travel, whether we agree on the purpose for which they travel," Mr. Kennedy said, groups and individuals like the Freedom Riders "should be able to move freely in interstate commerce."

He did not say whether he agreed with the purpose for which the Freedom Riders have said they were traveling.

Mr. Kennedy drew an analogy with freedom of the press.

"We may not like what people print in a paper," he said, "but there is no question about their constitutional right to print it. So that follows, in my opinion, for those who move in interstate commerce."

Such persons, he said "should enjoy the full constitutional protections given to them by the law and by the Constitution … I am hopeful that that will become the generally accepted view, and if there are any legal doubts about the right of people to move in interstate commerce, that that legal position will be clarified."

His own judgment, Mr. Kennedy said, is that "there is no question of the legal rights of the freedom travelers, freedom riders, that move in interstate commerce."

These comments appeared in sum to be the strongest Mr. Kennedy, as President, has made in the field of civil rights.

At a news conference on March 8, he said he would send civil rights legislation to Congress only "when I believe that we can usefully move ahead" through such bills.

On March 23, at a news conference, he cited what his Administration was doing through executive action, and put emphasis on the fields of equal job opportunity and voting rights.

Again, at his conference May 5, in commenting on the sacrifices he was asking of the American people, Mr. Kennedy said that "each person could come closer to the constitutional concept of equal opportunities for all Americans, regardless of race or creed."

In his campaign last year, Mr. Kennedy said it was the President's job to provide "moral and persuasive leadership" in civil rights. He was running on a platform that pledged, among other things, "equal access for all Americans to all areas of community life … including public facilities."

189 Riders Appeal Jackson Conviction

BY RICHARD H. PARKE | AUG. 15, 1961

JACKSON, MISS., AUG. 14 — One hundred and eighty-nine Freedom Riders appeared in the Hinds County Court today to appeal their convictions for breach of the peace.

They came by bus, train and plane from all parts of the country. All had been arrested in recent weeks for challenging racial barriers here. They had been released in $500 bond each, most of them after having served a portion of their sentences.

Judge Russel Moore began the proceedings in the heavily guarded court house by setting next Tuesday for the opening of arguments.

He announced, with the consent of attorneys for both sides, that he would dispose of the appeals on what amounted to virtually a day-to-day basis. He said he would hear two cases a day, with some exceptions, until a final session, now scheduled for Jan. 18, 1962.

The first week, beginning Tuesday, should, in the opinion of court observers, set the pattern for the defense arguments, and could result in a curtailment of the long schedule.

Only four defendants are to appear next week. Two, Henry Thomas, 19 years old, a Howard University student, and Julie Aaron, 20, of New Orleans, will appear on Tuesday. Joseph Carter, 22, of 98 Liberty Avenue, Brooklyn, and John Robert Lewis, 21, of Troy, Ala., are scheduled to appear Thursday. All are Negroes.

The two-a-day schedule prevails generally thereafter, except for time out to enable the defense to appear in Federal Court here. The cases of five of the Freedom Riders have been transferred there by petition.

William M. Kunstler, special counsel for the Congress of Racial Equality, said the defense would cite the Federal Judiciary Act, which provides that civil rights cases may come under Federal jurisdiction. The defense must prove, however, that testing segregation facilities involves a question of civil rights.

In Jackson, 1,500 people attended a N. A. A. C. P. nighttime rally, among them some 170 Freedom Riders in town to appeal previous convictions before the August term of Hinds County Court. James Farmer, of New York, National Director of CORE, gave the main address of the rally.

The appeal hearings beginning here next week will take the form of trials, since the municipal court in which the defendants were convicted originally is not a court of record. Thus the cases will be explored from every legal angle.

The defense is understood to be planning to base its arguments on two points of law. One is a Supreme Court decision in a Richmond, Va., case, the other an attack on two Mississippi laws governing breach of the peace.

In the Richmond case, the court last winter overturned the conviction of Bruce Boynton, a Negro law student, for staging a sit-in at a restaurant. Mr. Boynton was arrested under a state breach-of-peace law, but the Supreme Court ruled that the law had been invoked in his case to maintain segregation in interstate travel facilities.

The attacks on the Mississippi laws — one of which covers single arrests and the other group arrests — will be based chiefly on the contention that the Legislature enacted the statutes particularly to preserve segregation.

ENACTED IN 1960

They were enacted in the spring of 1960, when sit-in demonstrations were occurring in many Southern states.

Among the defendants here today were Mark Lane, Democratic Assemblyman of Manhattan. Mr. Lane, who was arrested for attempting to use segregated rest room facilities at the air terminal here, did not appear in court. He came before Judge Moore in chambers this morning and was told to return at 9 A.M. on Nov. 7.

At least 100 of the Riders are still serving jail terms, ranging as much as four months, in the city jail and in the state penitentiary at Parchman. Judge Moore had summoned a total of 198 defendants for today's hearings. Three of these have been in jail in New Orleans and were reported to be on their way here. The other six were not accounted for.

I.C.C. Orders End of Racial Curbs on Bus Travelers

BY JOSEPH A. LOFTUS | SEPT. 23, 1961

WASHINGTON, SEPT. 22 — The Interstate Commerce Commission prescribed rules today forbidding racial discrimination in interstate bus transportation. The rules cover terminal facilities as well as buses.

The commission thus granted a petition filed on May 29 by Attorney General Robert F. Kennedy.

"The time has come for this commission," Mr. Kennedy then asserted, "to declare unequivocally by regulation that a Negro passenger is free to travel the length and breadth of this country in the same manner as any other passenger."

The Attorney General's petition followed incidents involving Freedom Riders in several Southern states last spring.

DISPLAY OF SIGNS REQUIRED

Beginning Nov. 1, buses holding common carrier certificates issued by the I. C. C. must display signs saying:

"Seating aboard this vehicle is without regard to race, color, creed, or national origin, by order of the Interstate Commerce Commission."

The signs will be required until Jan. 1, 1963, unless the time is further extended by the commission.

On and after Jan. 1, 1963, a similar notice must be printed on all tickets sold for transportation in interstate or foreign commerce. The effective date of this regulation was put off until 1963 because tickets for the intervening period probably have been printed.

In addition, terminals serving interstate buses will be required to post the commission's new regulations.

Beginning Nov. 1, interstate carriers will be forbidden to use terminal facilities that segregate travelers by race.

"We find," the commission said, "that in a substantial part of the United States many Negro interstate passengers are subjected to racial segregation in several forms. On vehicles, they continue to be subjected to segregated seating based upon race.

"In many motor passenger terminals, Negro interstate passengers are compelled to use eating, rest room and other terminal facilities which are segregated."

In considering terminals and facilities, the commission said that the rule "would not be applicable, for example, to every independently operated roadside restaurant at which a bus stops solely to pick up or discharge occasional passengers, or to every independently operated corner drug store which sells tickets for a motor carrier."

"Where a carrier's ticket agent does nothing more for the benefit of the carrier's passengers than sell tickets and post schedules," the commission said, "we would not consider his place of business to be a terminal facility."

The rules would apply, however, where the agent "offers or provides facilities for the comfort and convenience of passengers, such as a public waiting room, rest room, or eating facilities."

Interstate passengers using common facilities may not be subjected to any inquiry as to whether they are traveling in intrastate or interstate commerce, the commission said.

The rules will require interstate bus operators to report to the commission any interference with the observance of the regulations.

Common carriers that violate the new regulations, or fail to report interference with the regulations, would be subject to penalties imposed by the commission. Fines for first violations will range from $100 to $500. Hereafter the range would be $200 to $500.

The commission has its own staff of investigators. Some types of alleged violations are turned over to the Department of Justice. The commission has no jurisdiction over local police officers. Thus any interference by them in the I. C. C. regulations would presumably be turned over to the Justice Department.

The commission, in 1955, consonant with the Supreme Court's school integration decision in the preceding year, ruled that discrimination in railroad passenger travel violated the law.

VIOLATION OF LAW FOUND

At the same time the commission declared that racial discrimination in bus transportation also violated the Interstate Commerce Act. Last year, the Supreme Court found that the refusal of service to a Negro bus passenger at a terminal lunch counter reserved for white persons violated the Interstate Commerce Act.

There has been no conflict between the conclusions of the commission and of the Supreme Court. The commission, however, issued no regulations to implement its findings. It received and investigated complaints on a case-by-case basis. Ten cases have been referred to United States attorneys with recommendations for criminal prosecution.

Air travel is not subject to the F. C. C.'s jurisdiction. However, the Justice Department has suits pending at New Orleans and Montgomery, Ala., to bring about desegregation at airport facilities at those cities.

The commission's decision today cited the ten cases sent to the Federal attorneys but did not report their outcome.

However, the commission said that "the record here shows that segregation has been practiced on such a regular basis as to convince us that case-by-case action initiated by individual complaints under Section 216 (E), standing alone, is not an adequate remedy."

"Accordingly," the commission went on, "we conclude that the prescription of general regulations directed to interstate motor common carriers of passengers over whom we have jurisdiction is warranted to supplement the remedy provided by Section 216 (E)."

Bus Depots Vary in Racial Policy

BY WILL LISSNER | NOV. 12, 1961

FREEDOM RIDERS WHO tested bus-terminal service in the South in the last ten days found a wide variety of conditions, the Congress of Racial Equality reported last week.

The tests were made to check compliance with the order of the Interstate Commerce Commission that all interstate transportation facilities be desegregated. The order took effect Nov. 1.

A state-by-state survey of conditions found by the bi-racial C. O. R. E. teams showed the following:

Alabama — The teams were served at most places and used unsegregated facilities in such communities as Anniston, Birmingham and Winfield. But they found no I. C. C. signs ordering desegregation. The posting of such signs was part of the commission's orders.

Arkansas — Served in Forest City, Fort Smith, Little Rock, El Dorado, Hamburg and Waldo. No I. C. C. signs were posted.

Florida — Served at Greyhound and Trailways terminals in Tallahassee, Jacksonville and Mariana, but no I. C. C. signs were posted.

Georgia — After four arrests in Atlanta, served in Thomasville, Valdosta, Macon and Augusta without incident.

Kentucky — Served in Ashland, Lexington, Portsmouth and Richmond.

Louisiana — Facilities unsegregated in Eunice, Franklin, Jeanerette, Houma, Lake Charles, Morgan City, New Iberia, New Orleans, Opelousas and Raceland. The police enforced segregation or refused entrance to Negroes in Alexandria, Crowley, Hollingsworth, Kratz Springs, Layfayette, Monroe and Shreveport. A terminal restaurant was closed in Baton Rouge, and one in Kinder was operated "privately" for whites.

Mississippi — Served in Greenville. Station closed "for repairs" in Hamilton and Tupelo. Segregation enforced, with or without

I. C. C. signs, in Granada, Greenwood, Jackson, Meridian, Natchez, New Albany, Winona, Sardis, Vicksburg and Winfield.

North Carolina — No discrimination in Fayetteville and Hamlet. Discrimination practiced in Wadesboro before and after removal of I. C. C. signs.

Oklahoma — Served in Oklahoma City and Seminole, refused service in MacAlester.

South Carolina — Columbia, Charleston, Greenville, Rockhill and Sumter unsegregated. Camden segregated one day, unsegregated the next. Negroes refused admittance to restaurant in Florence. Segregation continued in Lancaster.

Tennessee — Jackson, Memphis, Nashville and Union City unsegregated. Linden continued segregation.

Texas — No segregation encountered in Orange, Belmont, Gainesville, Sherman and Texarkana.

West Virginia — No segregation in Charleston and Huntington.

5 Negroes Beaten by Mississippi Mob

BY CLAUDE SITTON | NOV. 30, 1961

Riders attacked in McComb — crowd shouts 'Kill 'em.'

MCCOMB, MISS., NOV. 29 — A mob of cursing whites, shouting "Kill 'em! Kill 'em!" set upon five Negro Freedom Riders today and drove them from the Greyhound bus station.

Although the three youths and two girls were mauled severely, none was seriously injured. They fled to safety at a Negro hotel after escaping from their assailants in two taxis and a truck.

McComb policemen escorted the Freedom Riders to the bus terminal tonight and placed them aboard the New Orleans Express while Federal Bureau of Investigation agents looked on. This prevented the Negroes from making a second attempt to seek service at the lunch counter.

A dozen white youths and men in the small but angry crowd joined in pummeling the Negroes. They chased them around and over counters and tables in the waiting room of the terminal before kicking them out the door.

The mob tossed one youth into the air again and again in the street outside, kicking and beating him as he struck the pavement.

Five minutes after the Negroes had escaped, Chief of Police George Guy and Patrolman Edward Smith arrived from the City Hall, less than a block from the terminal. They cleared the streets and sidewalks with little trouble.

Johann Rush, a freelance television camera man from Jackson, was attacked this morning in an unrelated incident while taking film of the station and a group of whites standing around it.

The violence marked the first move in Mississippi's history to comply with a Federal court desegregation order. The Riders came here by bus this morning to test the city's compliance with a Federal directive to halt the enforcement of segregation at bus and rail terminals.

The order was handed down in open court last week and filed Monday in Jackson, the state capital. A United States Deputy Marshal served copies of it on Mayor C. H. Douglas, Chief Guy and the city's selectmen yesterday.

Agents of the Federal Bureau of Investigation, who were already here apparently as observers, began an immediate inquiry.

Officials of the Justice Department in Washington were also seeking to learn details of the outbreak.

The mob action here repeated on a smaller scale the riots that greeted Freedom Riders last May in Anniston, Birmingham and Montgomery, Ala.

Today's group, all members of the New Orleans chapter of the Congress of Racial Equality, said a further attempt would be made to use previously white terminal facilities.

"We'll be back," declared Doratha Smith, 18 years old, after she had been examined by Dr. James Anderson.

The five Negroes came here under the leadership of Jerome Smith, 22, president of the New Orleans chapter of the congress. The others are George Raymond, 18, Thomas Valentine, 23, and Alice Thompson, 22.

Their first effort to enter the terminal was unsuccessful. Shortly before they arrived this morning, the station agent reported a gas leak in the building. The Negroes were warned when they approached the door that it would be dangerous to enter.

"Well, wasn't that a coincidence," remarked Charles Gordon, a city selectman and member of the Citizens' Council, a segregationist group.

The weather was sunny but brisk as small knots of whites and Negroes gathered along the sidewalks of Canal Street near the pink stucco terminal. Youths in duck-tail haircuts and blue jeans crossed and recrossed the street from the terminal to the "City Billiard Parlor and Dominoes."

No policeman was in sight when the five Freedom Riders arrived in a taxi and walked up to the glass-jalousied entrance of the white waiting room.

An elderly white man in a gray felt hat and work-stained clothes blocked the way and sought to persuade them not to enter. But he stepped aside and the five filed into the joint, waiting room and cafe, past the brightly lighted pinball machines and back to the lunch counter in the rear.

Mr. Smith walked over to the ticket window and the four other Negroes took seats at the lunch counter. Mr. Raymond asked twice in a firm voice for service. He was ignored.

A. P. McGehee, operator of the bus terminal, walked behind the counter. Tapping his finger on the counter for emphasis, he told each of the Negroes:

"Greyhound does not own this building; Greyhound does not own this restaurant. You get out of here."

At this point, a youth grabbed a half-filled cup of coffee from a table and walked rapidly down the line of stools at the counter. When he reached Mr. Raymond, he struck him sharply at the base of the skull with the cup and saucer, spilling coffee over the Negro's head and back.

Mr. Smith then waved to the four others to join him in a row of seats at the front of the waiting room. As they got up to move, a short, wiry white man of about 35 jumped at the Negro leader and began beating him with his fists.

The Negro doubled over and ducked his head under a rain of blows to the back of the neck, the shoulder and the stomach. "I'll kill him! I'll kill him! I'll kill him!" yelled the white.

The assailants then shoved and kicked the youths and the two girls through the door. They fled on to the sidewalk and out into the street, where their taxi stood waiting.

Both Mayor Douglas and Chief Guy had asserted to newsmen that no further attempt would be made to enforce segregation in waiting rooms.

Supreme Court Reaffirms Ban on Travel Segregation

BY E. W. KENWORTHY | FEB. 27, 1962

WASHINGTON, FEB. 26 — The Supreme Court ordered a Federal court in Mississippi today to uphold quickly the right of Negroes to unsegregated transportation service. The case came to the Supreme Court on appeal after a special three-judge Federal court in Jackson, Miss., refused to rule on the constitutionality of state and local laws requiring segregation in trains, buses, street cars, terminal waiting rooms and restaurants.

The special panel said that the meaning of these laws should first be determined by state courts that are now considering several Freedom Rider cases.

Today the Supreme Court, in a brief, unsigned opinion, said in effect that the anti-segregation principle had been established in prior decisions.

OPINION BY THE COURT

The Supreme Court said:

"We have settled beyond question that no state may require racial segregation of interstate or intrastate transportation facilities."

Since the question "is no longer open," the court said that there had been no need to convene the three-judge court. Under Federal law, such a tribunal is convened only when an injunction is sought to prevent enforcement of a state statute on the ground of its unconstitutionality.

"There is no such ground," the Supreme Court stated, "when the constitutional issue presented is essentially fictitious."

The court found this issue fictitious because "prior decisions" had made "frivolous any claim that a state statute on its face is not unconstitutional."

Therefore, the court annulled the judgment of the three-judge court. It remanded the case to the district court to be heard by one judge with instructions "for expeditious disposition, in the light of this opinion, of the [Negroes'] claims of right to unsegregated transportation service."

The lawsuit was filed in June, 1961, by three Negroes, Samuel Bailey, Joseph Broadwater and Burnett L. Jacob. They asked for injunctions requiring officials of the state of Mississippi, the city of Jackson and several common carriers to stop enforcing segregation laws and ordinances.

FREEDOM RIDER CASES

The Negroes also sought an injunction to stay prosecution of the Freedom Riders for violating segregation statutes or "breach of the peace" laws.

At the request of the Negroes, the three-judge court was convened. Two of the members, District Judges Sidney C. Mize and Claude F. Clayton, handed down the decision postponing further proceedings. Appeals Judge Richard T. Rives dissented, arguing that officials should be ordered to stop enforcing segregation laws and that the Freedom Rider suits should be blocked.

About 220 riders have been arrested since the filing of the case.

Last Dec. 18 the Supreme Court refused to order a temporary stay in the prosecution of the Freedom Riders. In the opinion today, the court said the plaintiffs lacked "standing" to enjoin the prosecutions because they themselves had not been arrested or prosecuted. They "cannot represent a class of whom they are not a part," the court said.

LEGAL STUDY PLANNED

However, the court said that, "as passengers using the segregated transportation facilities," the three Negroes "are aggrieved parties and have standing to enforce their rights to nonsegregated treatment."

At the Justice Department, a spokesman said that Government attorneys would immediately begin a study of the court action because of its possible effect on suits filed in eight other cases of travel segregation in the South.

These suits grew out of regulations issued last Sept. 22 by the Interstate Commerce Commission, prohibiting discrimination against bus passengers both while they are traveling and at terminals.

Counsel for the Negroes were Constance Baker Motley, Jack Greenberg and James M. Nabrit 3d, all members of the legal staff of the Legal Defense and Educational Fund of the National Association for the Advancement of Colored People.

Joe T. Patterson, Attorney General of Mississippi, conducted the case for the defense.

CHAPTER 3

Martin Luther King Jr. and Coretta Scott King

The Rev. Dr. Martin Luther King Jr. and Coretta Scott King were the most influential couple of the civil rights movement. He was able to rouse a crowd with his impassioned, thought-provoking speeches, and became a symbol of nonviolent protests and how they could inspire change. She was a dedicated mother to their children, and an activist in her own right who marched and protested alongside her husband. After Dr. King's death, Coretta vigilantly continued to fight not only for racial equality, but for other marginalized communities as well, carrying on her husband's legacy as a defender of the oppressed.

President Urged to End Race Laws

BY THE NEW YORK TIMES | JUNE 6, 1961

THE REV. DR. MARTIN LUTHER KING JR., head of the Southern Christian Leadership Conference, called on President Kennedy yesterday to issue a "second Emancipation Proclamation" striking down all racial segregation laws.

"The time has now come," he said, "for the President of the United States to issue a firm Executive Order declaring all forms of racial segregation illegal."

At a press conference at the Sheraton-Atlantic Hotel in New York, Dr. King asserted that Negroes today were no longer willing to put up with "meaningless delays and a crippling gradualism."

The Rev. Wyatt Tee Walker, executive director of the leadership conference, said later that this was the first time a leading Negro spokesman for the integration movement had called for an immediate end to all segregation laws.

"There is a mighty stirring in this land," Dr. King said. "The sit-ins at lunch counters and Freedom Riders on buses are making it palpably clear that segregation must end and that it must end soon."

LEGALITY IS IN DOUBT

There is some question as to whether the President has the power to issue such a sweeping Executive Order ending all segregation laws.

Herbert Wechsler, Harlan Fiske Stone Professor of Constitutional Law at Columbia University, said that the President "could not change the legal situation by issuing such an order."

Professor Wechsler said that Abraham Lincoln made his Emancipation Proclamation ending slavery "under wartime powers" and that until passage of the Thirteenth Amendment there were "grave doubts" as to its legality.

"We are determined," he said, "to launch a large-scale assault on all systems of segregation, including fly-ins at interstate airports."

Dr. King urged the President or Vice President Johnson to visit the deep South to "show that the full weight of the Federal Government is morally behind the integration movement."

Dr. King Opening Negro Vote Drive

BY RALPH KATZ | SEPT. 26, 1961

THE REV. DR. MARTIN LUTHER KING said last night that a campaign to dou-
ble the number of Negro voters in the South this fall was under way
and would be pressed hard.

He said there would be "stand-ins by hundreds of people who will
present their bodies and lives at places of registration determined to
register and vote." He said he expected opposition, but that hundreds
of students had been mobilized in rural and city areas in the campaign
for votes.

The movement, he said, began two weeks ago after having been
approved by the executive committee of the Southern Christian Leadership Conference, of which Dr. King is president.

ADDRESSES HOSPITAL UNION

Dr. King described the new Southern Negro campaign to a meeting of
600 members of Local 1199 of the Drug and Hospital Employees Union
at the Diplomat Hotel, 108 West Forty-third Street in New York. His
audience, mostly Negroes and Puerto Rican hospital workers, listened
to him raptly and cheered loudly.

He said that, of 5,000,000 Negroes in Southern states eligible to
vote, only 1,300,000 were registered. He conceded that there were
some too lazy or unconcerned to register. But, he added, "thousands
and millions faced external resistance to their registration."

He said that the campaign to register and vote was not one of "hate
and violence" but a determination to be "free."

"We are willing to suffer, sacrifice and die, if necessary, to make
that freedom a reality," he continued.

Dr. King recalled the struggles and the jailings of Freedom Riders.
He said that the recent ruling of the Interstate Commerce Commission

that no bus facilities may be segregated after Nov. 1 showed that the struggle had not been in vain.

He declared that he would never be satisfied until Negroes had won equality in all aspects of American life, and that the fight was one "to save the soul of the nation."

Mayor Wagner shared the platform and the topic — segregation — with Mr. King.

The Mayor spoke of the "hidden enemy" in the city. He said that person was the one who professed to be without prejudice, but who exercised discrimination against Negroes and Puerto Ricans.

The Mayor drew prolonged applause when he told the hospital workers that he included employees of voluntary hospitals among workers for whom he was seeking to obtain a minimum wage rate of $1.50 an hour.

Many of these unskilled workers now are paid $1.12 ½ an hour, according to the union.

Dr. King Is Freed

SPECIAL TO THE NEW YORK TIMES | DEC. 19, 1961

ALBANY, GA., DEC. 18 — An agreement was reached today in this city's racial controversy. It paved the way for the release of the Rev. Dr. Martin Luther King Jr. and about 300 other Negroes from prison.

Dr. King, head of the Southern Christian Leadership Conference, left jail after a $400 security bond had been posted for him.

Others among the 750 persons arrested during five mass demonstrations last week were brought here from jails in surrounding counties tonight and were going through the bonding process.

The agreement brought relief to Negroes, but little enthusiasm. A leader said:

"It's nothing to shout to the rafters about."

The plan calls for ending mass protests and an organized boycott against white merchants.

Negroes also agreed to wait at least a month before initiating new negotiations on their demands for lowering racial barriers and obtaining better job opportunities.

In return for these concessions, Mayor Asa D. Kelley and other city officials agreed to take the following steps:

• Assure police compliance with an Interstate Commerce Commission ruling against segregation in bus and rail terminals.

• Release all prisoners who are property owners, or can show evidence of employment, on signature bonds.

• Reduce bonds for two local Freedom Riders facing a state charge of unlawful assembly from $750 to $200 and for eight other riders from outside the community from $1,000 to $400.

• Give the Albany movement an opportunity to present its demands for other changes in racial customs to the new City Commission Jan. 11.

The Rev. Dr. King waiting in the Albany, Ga., chief of police's office following his arrest last week.

Charges filed against the demonstrators for parading without a permit, congregating on a sidewalk and obstructing traffic will be held in abeyance at the discretion of the police chief. It was indicated that they would not be revived except on renewal of the demonstrations.

Marion S. Page, secretary of the Albany movement, announced the terms to an overflow meeting at the Shiloh Baptist Church. He termed them a "first step."

Chief of Police Laurie Pritchett has agreed to accompany him to the commission meeting and recommend that the seven-member body consider the Negroes other demands, according to Mr. Page.

Mayor Kelley, Chief Pritchett, Mr. Page and Donald L. Hollowell, an Atlanta lawyer retained by the Student Nonviolent Coordinating Committee, worked out the plan in talks that began at 9:30 A.M. and ended at 4:30 P.M.

Whites expressed satisfaction over the outcome of the negotiations and that no violence had erupted in this southwestern Georgia city of 56,000.

Chief Pritchett said the Negroes had been promised nothing that marked a departure from the city's established policies.

The remarks of some leaders seemed intended to convey the impression to white residents that no concessions had been made. While this was not wholly true, it appeared that the concessions were minor.

There was considerable doubt among observers, based on private comments by white leaders that a renewal of negotiations would bring major gains for Negroes unless accompanied by pressure.

Dr. King reversed his previous refusal to be released by posting bond. He indicated he was less than satisfied with the plan.

However, he said, as a result of talks with W. G. Anderson, chairman of the Albany Movement, it seemed the practical course to take.

"I would not want to stand in the way of meaningful negotiations," he said.

Mr. Anderson, who was arrested with Dr. King Saturday while the two led a march on the city hall, signed both their bonds.

Leaders of organizations in the Negro protest movement met today in a show of unity. A split in their ranks had become apparent yesterday.

At the meeting were officers of the National Association for the Advancement of Colored People, the Southern Christian Leadership Conference, which Dr. King heads, and the Student Nonviolent Coordinating Committee.

"If there was an indication of division, it grew out of a breakdown of communications," Dr. King declared after his release. "The unity is far greater than our inevitable points of disagreement."

Spokesman for Negroes

SPECIAL TO THE NEW YORK TIMES | JULY 16, 1962

ATLANTA, JULY 15 — Since 1956, when he headed the Negroes' highly successful bus boycott In Montgomery, Ala., the Rev. Dr. Martin Luther King Jr. has seen his power and prestige approach the dimensions of Booker T. Washington. Lately, however, some of his difficulties have also become more visible. Dr. King first emerged as a spokesman for his people, a role in which he was able to articulate and dramatize the Negroes' cause. But today he is forced to serve as an administrator, fund-raiser, mediator and politician. And he concedes that the results of some of his efforts in these latter fields have been less than satisfactory.

"He's woefully inadequate in organizational ability," one Southern Negro leader said.

Others blame his friends for some of his current problems. Ambitious lieutenants within the Southern Christian Leadership Conference, of which Dr. King is president, are said to have made comments and taken actions that have incurred the anger of officials of the National Association for the Advancement of Colored People. Other aides of Dr. King, acting without his authorization, agreed to a Hollywood proposal that he play the role of a Georgia Senator in the movie version of "Advise and Consent." This involved Dr. King in a controversy that ended with an awkward withdrawal.

DISPUTE ON CHARTER PLEA

He became involved recently in another dispute after having made a call to a Federal Home Loan Bank official in Washington to support the application of a group in Miami, Fla., for a savings and loan association charter. He said that he did not know at the time that another group was seeking the charter.

He demonstrated his awareness of the controversial position he occupies only last week in a speech to the N. A. A. C. P. convention here in Atlanta. He contended that civil rights leaders were being "victimized" by sensational accounts of their differences.

"We are enticed into self-serving statements and borderline slander about others to furnish gossip and colorful copy," he said.

Those who heard him were only too well aware that some of Dr. King's own subordinates had been as guilty of this as leaders in other organizations, in some instances calling the association a "black bourgeois club" and worse.

Although speaking engagements take him around the country and even out of it, Dr. King still must try to maintain some supervision of the activities of a growing staff here at the leadership conference headquarters.

Because of his dependence on gifts to keep his organization going, he must listen to conflicting advice from his benefactors regarding strategy. His chief problem is that he must seek to project an image of the conference that differs from that of the N. A. A. C. P. and the Congress of Racial Equality and thus justify its existence.

Yet few will dispute Dr. King's success as a spokesman for the Negro. And perhaps his political power was demonstrated in 1960 when, while he was serving a jail sentence, John F. Kennedy telephoned Mrs. King to express concern for the Negro leader.

Political experts said this telephone call enhanced the Democratic nominee's standing with Negro voters and perhaps decided his election to the Presidency.

Martin Luther King Jr. was born on Jan. 15, 1929, in Atlanta, the son of the pastor of the Ebenezer Baptist Church. The future leader's maternal grandfather, the Rev. A. D. Williams, turned Ebenezer Baptist Church into one of the leading houses of worship for Atlanta Negroes.

Dr. King was an active servant in the cause of integration almost from the time he left Boston University in 1954 with a doctorate in systematic theology. He had little more than arrived in Montgomery, Ala., to fill his first pastorate when the bus boycott there began in December 1955.

A Federal court desegregation order rather than the boycott, ended the dispute in December, 1956.

From Montgomery, Dr. King tested his version of passive resistance and nonviolence elsewhere in the South, and personally demonstrated what he meant by his code.

"It may mean going to jail," he wrote. "If such is the case, the resister must be willing to fill the jailhouses of the South. It may even mean physical death. But if physical death is the price that a man must pay to free his children and his White brethren from a permanent death of the spirit, then nothing could be more redemptive."

Dr. King is a small man with a broad, sloping face and heavily muscled neck and shoulders that give an appearance of power to his 5-foot 8-inch frame. He expresses himself quietly and eloquently; there is no arrogance about him, nor any intellectual posturing. He lives in a modest, rented frame house with his wife, Coretta, a daughter and a son.

Negroes to Rally Today in Georgia

BY CLAUDE SITTON | JULY 21, 1962

Dr. King to risk jail again — 300 to 500 expected.

ALBANY, GA., JULY 20 — The city government was told today that 300 to 500 Negroes would stage a mass demonstration tomorrow in front of the City Hall.

The Rev. Dr. Martin Luther King said he would participate in the demonstration to protest the refusal of city commissioners to negotiate a dispute over racial issues. He said he was willing to return to jail if necessary.

The minister told a singing, praying, foot-stamping rally of 1,200 Negroes tonight at Third Kiokee Baptist Church to "get on your walking shoes."

Chief of Police Laurie Pritchett said "if they violate any laws they're going to jail." His remark, which came, after a round of hurried conferences with city officials, indicated that a decision had been made to block the protest.

Officials learned of the demonstration in a letter from W. G. Anderson. He is an osteopath who is president of the Albany Movement, an anti-segregation group.

The letter, addressed to Stephen A. Roos, the city manager, asked police assistance but did not request a parade permit. Dr. King, Dr. Anderson, 263 other Negroes and one white youth were arrested last Dec. 16 for failing to get such a permit before staging a march toward the City Hall.

Dr. King was imprisoned for two days last week after being convicted of violating the parade ordinance in the December demonstration. This led to the renewal of a racial controversy of long standing in this southwestern Georgia city.

The city attorney, Henry Grady Rawls, flew to Atlanta today and conferred with Henry Neal, legal aide to Gov. S. Ernest Vandiver. It was understood that they had discussed court action to expel Dr. King from Albany.

POLICE STANDING BY

More than 160 city policemen, state highway patrolmen, state revenue agents and sheriff's deputies from surrounding counties were standing by here. Mayor Asa D. Kelley has said that Governor Vandiver had promised to call out national guardsmen immediately upon request.

Two groups of Negroes failed today in attempts to desegregate a public park and a drug store lunch counter.

A police official ordered the lunch counter at Lee's Drug Store closed down shortly before seven teen-age Negroes arrived. The demonstrators entered the store but left when the manager shouted, "Get out! Get out! I don't want you in here!"

Eight others were ordered to leave when they tried to use the swimming pool at Tallulah Massey Park.

Dr. King returned here from Washington by plane this afternoon. He spoke tonight at a mass meeting called by the Albany Movement and its supporters in the Third Kiokee Baptist Church.

Dr. Anderson's letter to the city manager emphasized that tomorrow's demonstration, set for late afternoon, would be a peaceful one.

He said that participants would leave from Shiloh and Mount Zion Baptist Churches, which are four blocks from the center of the business section, and would observe all traffic signals.

"The group would welcome assistance by the Albany Police Department in facilitating the crossing of streets," the letter said.

PRAYER SERVICE PLANNED

"In the general vicinity of city hall, a prayer service will be conducted, followed by oral statements by one or more of the group. This total service will not exceed one hour," the letter continued.

"The purpose of this gathering is to manifest in the presence of God, the Albany community and the world our great concern over the inability of Negro citizens of Albany to effectively communicate to the city fathers their community problems," the letter said.

Aside from the Commissioners' refusal to meet with Negro leaders, the chief issue in the dispute is the demand that all charges be dropped against the more than 800 persons arrested in demonstrations beginning last December.

The controversy here dates back to February, 1961, when the Negroes asked for the establishment of a committee to hear their complaints about segregation and such matters as unpaved streets.

The arrest of a group of Freedom Riders at a rail terminal in December touched off the demonstrations.

Chief Pritchett has contended that his men no longer enforce segregation at bus and rail stations here. But the Negroes have replied that sporadic harassment has continued.

Dr. King, who joined the Albany Movement here by invitation in December, summed up the attitude of its leaders in a news conference after his arrival from Atlanta.

"We have sought to negotiate with the City Commission," he said. "We sent them two telegrams. And it seems that the response has been negative through and through."

200,000 March for Civil Rights in Orderly Washington Rally; President Sees Gain for Negro

BY E. W. KENWORTHY | AUG. 29, 1963

WASHINGTON, AUG. 28 — More than 200,000 Americans, most of them black but many of them white, demonstrated here today for a full and speedy program of civil rights and equal job opportunities.

It was the greatest assembly for a redress of grievances that this capital has ever seen.

One hundred years and 240 days after Abraham Lincoln enjoined the emancipated slaves to "abstain from all violence" and "labor faithfully for reasonable wages," this vast throng proclaimed in march and song and through the speeches of their leaders that they were still waiting for the freedom, and the jobs.

CHILDREN CLAP AND SING

There was no violence to mar the demonstration. In fact, at times there was an air of hootenanny about it as groups of schoolchildren clapped hands and swung into the familiar freedom songs.

But if the crowd was good-natured, the underlying tone was one of dead seriousness. The emphasis was on "freedom" and "now." At the same time the leaders emphasized, paradoxically but realistically, that the struggle was just beginning.

On Capitol Hill, opinion was divided about the impact of the demonstration in stimulating Congressional action on civil rights legislation. But at the White House, President Kennedy declared that the cause of 20,000,000 Negroes had been advanced by the march.

The march leaders went from the shadows of the Lincoln Memorial to the White House to meet with the President for 75 minutes. Afterward, Mr. Kennedy issued a 400-word statement praising the marchers for the "deep fervor and the quiet dignity" that had characterized the demonstration.

SAYS NATION CAN BE PROUD

The nation, the President said, "can properly be proud of the demonstration that has occurred here today."

The main target of the demonstration was Congress, where committees are now considering the Administration's civil rights bill.

At the Lincoln Memorial this afternoon, some speakers, knowing little of the ways of Congress, assumed that the passage of a strengthened civil rights bill had been assured by the moving events of the day.

But from statements by Congressional leaders, after they had met with the march committee this morning, this did not seem certain at all. These statements came before the demonstration.

Senator Mike Mansfield of Montana, the Senate Democratic leader, said he could not say whether the mass protest would speed the legislation, which faces a filibuster by Southerners.

Senator Everett McKinley Dirksen of Illinois, the Republican leader, said he thought the demonstration would be neither an advantage nor a disadvantage to the prospects for the civil rights bill.

The human tide that swept over the Mall between the shrines of Washington and Lincoln fell back faster than it came on. As soon as the ceremony broke up this afternoon, the exodus began. With astounding speed, the last buses and trains cleared the city by mid-evening.

At 9 P.M. the city was as calm as the waters of the Reflecting Pool between the two memorials.

At the Lincoln Memorial early in the afternoon, in the midst of a songfest before the addresses, Josephine Baker, the singer, who had flown from her home in Paris, said to the thousands stretching down both sides of the Reflecting Pool:

"You are on the eve of a complete victory. You can't go wrong. The world is behind you."

Marchers assembling around the Reflecting Pool at the Lincoln Memorial.

Miss Baker said, as if she saw a dream coming true before her eyes, that "this is the happiest day of my life."

But of all the 10 leaders of the march on Washington who followed her, only the Rev. Dr. Martin Luther King Jr., president of the Southern Christian Leadership Conference, saw that dream so hopefully.

The other leaders, except for the three clergymen among the 10, concentrated on the struggle ahead and spoke in tough, even harsh, language.

But paradoxically it was Dr. King — who had suffered perhaps most of all — who ignited the crowd with words that might have been written by the sad, brooding man enshrined within.

As he arose, a great roar welled up from the crowd. When he started to speak, a hush fell.

"Even though we face the difficulties of today and tomorrow, I still have a dream," he said.

"It is a dream chiefly rooted in the American dream," he went on.

"I have a dream that one day this nation will rise up and live out the true meaning of its creed: "We hold these truths to be self-evident, that all men are created equal.'

DREAM OF BROTHERHOOD

"I have a dream…" The vast throng listening intently to him roared.

"… that one day on the red hills of Georgia, the sons of former slaves and the sons of former slave-owners will be able to sit together at the table of brotherhood.

"I have a dream…" The crowd roared.

"…that one day even the State of Mississippi, a state sweltering with the heat of injustice, sweltering with the heat of oppression, will be transformed into an oasis of freedom and justice.

"I have a dream…" The crowd roared.

"…that my four little children will one day live in a nation where they will not be judged by the color of their skin but by the content of their character.

"I have a dream…" The crowd roared.

"…that one day every valley shall be exalted, every hill and mountain shall be made low, the rough places will be made plain, and the crooked places will be made straight, and the glory of the Lord shall be revealed and all flesh shall see it together."

As Dr. King concluded with a quotation from a Negro hymn — "Free at last, free at last, thank God almighty" — the crowd, recognizing that he was finishing, roared once again and waved their signs and pennants.

But the civil rights leaders, who knew the strength of the forces arrayed against them from past battles, knew also that a hard struggle lay ahead. The tone of their speeches was frequently militant.

Roy Wilkins, executive secretary of the National Association for the Advancement of Colored People, made plain that he and his colleagues thought the President's civil rights bill did not go nearly far enough. He said:

"The President's proposals represent so moderate an approach that if any one is weakened or eliminated, the remainder will be little more than sugar water. Indeed, the package needs strengthening."

Harshest of all the speakers was John Lewis, chairman of the Student Nonviolent Coordinating Committee.

"My friends," he said, "let us not forget that we are involved in a serious social revolution. But by and large American politics is dominated by politicians who build their career on immoral compromising and ally themselves with open forums of political, economic and social exploitation."

He concluded:

"They're talking about slowdown and stop. We will not stop.

"If we do not get meaningful legislation out of this Congress, the time will come when we will not confine our marching to Washington. We will march through the South, through the streets of Jackson, through the streets of Danville, through the streets of Cambridge, through the streets of Birmingham.

"But we will march with the spirit of love and the spirit of dignity that we have shown here today."

In the original text of the speech, distributed last night, Mr. Lewis had said:

"We will not wait for the President, the Justice Department, nor the Congress, but we will take matters into our own hands and create a source of power, outside of any national structure, that could and would assure us a victory."

He also said in the original text that "we will march through the South, through the heart of Dixie, the way Sherman did."

It was understood that at least the last of these statements was changed as the result of a protest by the Most Rev. Patrick J. O'Boyle, Roman Catholic Archbishop of Washington, who refused to give the invocation if the offending words were spoken by Mr. Lewis.

The great day really began the night before. As a half moon rose over the lagoon by the Jefferson Memorial and the tall, lighted shaft of the Washington Monument gleamed in the reflecting pool, a file of Negroes from out of town began climbing the steps of the Lincoln Memorial.

There, while the carpenters nailed the last planks on the television platforms for the next day and the TV technicians called through the loud-speakers, "Final audio, one, two, three, four," a middle-aged Negro couple, the man's arm around the shoulders of his plump wife, stood and read with their lips:

"If we shall suppose that American slavery is one of the offenses which in the providence of God must needs come but which having continued through His appointed time, He now wills to remove. ..."

The day dawned clear and cool. At 7 A. M. the town had a Sunday appearance, except for the shuttle buses drawn up in front of Union Station, waiting.

By 10 A. M. there were 40,000 on the slopes around the Washington Monument. An hour later the police estimated the crowd at 90,000. And still they poured in.

Because some things went wrong at the monument, everything was right. Most of the stage and screen celebrities from New York and Hollywood who were scheduled to begin entertaining the crowd at 10 did not arrive at the airport until 11:15.

As a result the whole affair at the monument grounds began to take on the spontaneity of a church picnic. Even before the entertainment was to begin, groups of high school students were singing with wonderful improvisations and hand-clapping all over the monument slope.

Civil rights demonstrators who had been released from jail in Danville, Va., were singing:

Move on, move on,
Till all the world is free.

And members of Local 144 of the Hotel and Allied Service Employees Union from New York City, an integrated local since 1950, were stomping:

Oh, freedom, we shall not,
we shall not be moved,
Just like a tree that's
planted by the water.

Then the pros took over, starting with the folk singers. The crowd joined in with them.

Joan Baez started things rolling with "the song" — "We Shall Overcome."

Oh deep in my heart I do believe
We shall overcome some day.

And Peter, Paul and Mary sang "How many times must a man look up before he can see the sky."

And Odetta's great, full-throated voice carried almost to Capitol Hill: "If they ask you who you are, tell them you're a child of God."

Jackie Robinson told the crowd that "we cannot be turned back," and Norman Thomas, the venerable Socialist, said: "I'm glad I lived long enough to see this day."

The march to the Lincoln Memorial was supposed to start at 11:30, behind the leaders. But at 11:20 it set off spontaneously down Constitution Avenue behind the Kenilworth Knights, a local drum and bugle corps dazzling in yellow silk blazers, green trousers and green berets.

Apparently forgotten was the intention to make the march to the Lincoln Memorial a solemn tribute to Medgar W. Evers, N.A.A.C.P. official murdered in Jackson, Miss., last June 12, and others who had died for the cause of civil rights.

The leaders were lost, and they never did get to the head of the parade.

The leaders included also Walter P. Reuther, head of the United Automobile Workers; A. Philip Randolph, head of American Negro Labor Council; the Rev. Dr. Eugene Carson Blake, vice chairman of the Commission on Religion and Race of the National Council of Churches; Mathew Ahmann, executive director of the National Catholic

Conference for Interracial Justice; Rabbi Joachim Prinz, president of the American Jewish Congress; Whitney M. Young Jr., executive director of the National Urban League, and James Farmer, president of the Congress of Racial Equality.

All spoke at the memorial except Mr. Farmer, who is in jail in Louisiana following his arrest as a result of a civil rights demonstration. His speech was read by Floyd B. McKissick, CORE national chairman.

At the close of the ceremonies at the Lincoln Memorial, Bayard Rustin, the organizer of the march, asked Mr. Randolph, who conceived it, to lead the vast throng in a pledge.

Repeating after Mr. Randolph, the marchers pledged "complete personal commitment to the struggle for jobs and freedom for Americans" and "to carry the message of the march to my friends and neighbors back home and arouse them to an equal commitment and an equal effort."

Martin Luther King Jr.: Leader of Millions in Nonviolent Drive for Racial Justice

BY MURRAY SCHUMACH | APRIL 5, 1968

TO MANY MILLIONS of American Negroes, the Rev. Dr. Martin Luther King Jr. was the prophet of their crusade for racial equality. He was their voice of anguish, their eloquence in humiliation, their battle cry for human dignity. He forged for them the weapons of nonviolence that withstood and blunted the ferocity of segregation.

And to many millions of American whites, he was one of a group of Negroes who preserved the bridge of communication between races when racial warfare threatened the United States in the nineteen-sixties, as Negroes sought the full emancipation pledged to them a century before by Abraham Lincoln.

To the world Dr. King had the stature that accrued to a winner of the Nobel Peace Prize; a man with access to the White House and the Vatican; a veritable hero in the African states that were just emerging from colonialism.

BETWEEN EXTREMES

In his dedication to nonviolence, Dr. King was caught between white and Negro extremists as racial tensions erupted into arson, gunfire and looting in many of the nation's cities during the summer of 1967.

Militant Negroes, with the cry of, "burn, baby burn," argued that only by violence and segregation could the Negro attain self-respect, dignity and real equality in the United States.

Floyd B. McKissick, when director of the Congress of Racial Equality, declared in August of that year that it was a "foolish assumption to try to sell nonviolence to the ghettos."

And white extremists, not bothering to make distinctions between degrees of Negro militancy, looked upon Dr. King as one of their chief enemies.

At times in recent months, efforts by Dr. King to utilize nonviolent methods exploded into violence.

VIOLENCE IN MEMPHIS

Last week, when he led a protest march through downtown Memphis, Tenn., in support of the city's striking sanitation workers, a group of Negro youths suddenly began breaking store windows and looting, and one Negro was shot to death.

Two days later, however, Dr. King said he would stage another demonstration and attributed the violence to his own "miscalculation."

At the time he was assassinated in Memphis, Dr. King was involved in one of his greatest plans to dramatize the plight of the poor and stir Congress to help Negroes.

He called this venture the "Poor People's Campaign." It was to be a huge "camp-in" either in Washington or in Chicago during the Democratic National Convention.

In one of his last public pronouncements before the shooting, Dr. King told an audience in a Harlem church on March 26:

"We need an alternative to riots and to timid supplication. Nonviolence is our most potent weapon."

His strong beliefs in civil rights and nonviolence made him one of the leading opponents of American participation in the war in Vietnam. To him the war was unjust, diverting vast sums away from programs to alleviate the condition of the Negro poor in this country. He called the conflict "one of history's most cruel and senseless wars." Last January he said:

"We need to make clear in this political year, to Congressmen on both sides of the aisle and to the President of the United States that we will no longer vote for men who continue to see the killing of Vietnamese and Americans as the best way of advancing the goals of freedom and self-determination in Southeast Asia."

OBJECT OF MANY ATTACKS

Inevitably, as a symbol of integration, he became the object of unrelenting attacks and vilification. His home was bombed. He was spat upon and mocked. He was struck and kicked. He was stabbed, almost fatally, by a deranged Negro woman. He was frequently thrown into jail. Threats became so commonplace that his wife could ignore burning crosses on the lawn and ominous phone calls. Through it all he adhered to the creed of passive disobedience that infuriated segregationists.

The adulation that was heaped upon him eventually irritated even some Negroes in the civil rights movement who worked hard, but in relative obscurity. They pointed out — and Dr. King admitted — that he was a poor administrator. Sometimes, with sarcasm, they referred to him, privately, as "De Lawd." They noted that Dr. King's successes were built on the labors of many who had gone before him, the noncoms and privates of the civil rights army who fought without benefit of headlines and television cameras.

The Negro extremists he criticized were contemptuous of Dr. King. They dismissed his passion for nonviolence as another form of servility to white people. They called him an "Uncle Tom," and charged that he was hindering the Negro struggle for equality.

Dr. King's belief in nonviolence was subjected to intense pressure in 1966, when some Negro groups adopted the slogan "black power" in the aftermath of civil rights marches into Mississippi and race riots in Northern cities. He rejected the idea, saying:

"The Negro needs the white man to free him from his fears. The white man needs the Negro to free him from his guilt. A doctrine of black supremacy is as evil as a doctrine of white supremacy."

The doctrine of "black power" threatened to split the Negro civil rights movement and antagonize white liberals who had been supporting Negro causes, and Dr. King suggested "militant nonviolence" as a formula for progress with peace.

At the root of his civil rights convictions was an even more profound faith in the basic goodness of man and the great potential of American democracy. These beliefs gave to his speeches a fervor that could not be stilled by criticism.

Scores of millions of Americans — white as well as Negro — who sat before television sets in the summer of 1963 to watch the awesome march of some 200,000 Negroes on Washington were deeply stirred when Dr. King, in the shadow of the Lincoln Memorial, said:

"Even though we face the difficulties of today and tomorrow, I still have a dream. I have a dream that one day this nation will rise up and live out the true meaning of its creed: 'We hold these truths to be self-evident, that all men are created equal.' "

And all over the world, men were moved as they read his words of Dec. 10, 1964, when he became the third member of his race to receive the Nobel Peace Prize.

INSISTENT ON MAN'S DESTINY

"I refuse to accept the idea that man is mere flotsam and jetsam in the river of life which surrounds him," he said. "I refuse to accept the view that mankind is so tragically bound to the starless midnight of racism and war that the bright daybreak of peace and brotherhood can never become a reality.

"I refuse to accept the cynical notion that nation after nation must spiral down a militaristic stairway into the hell of thermonuclear destruction. I believe that unarmed, truth and unconditional love will have the final word in reality. This is why right, temporarily defeated, is stronger than evil triumphant."

For the poor and unlettered of his own race, Dr. King spoke differently. There he embraced the rhythm and passion of the revivalist and evangelist. Some observers of Dr. King's technique said that others in the movement were more effective in this respect. But Dr. King had the touch, as he illustrated in a church in Albany, Ga., in 1962:

"So listen to me, children: Put on your marching shoes; don'cha get weary; though the path ahead may be dark and dreary; we're walking for freedom, children."

Or there was the meeting in Gadsden, Ala., late in 1963, when he displayed another side of his ability before an audience of poor Negroes. It went as follows:

King: I hear they are beating you.

Audience: Yes, yes.

King: I hear they are cursing you.

Audience: Yes, yes.

King: I hear they are going into your homes and doing nasty things and beating you.

Audience: Yes, yes.

King: Some of you have knives, and I ask you to put them up. Some of you have arms, and I ask you to put them up. Get the weapon of nonviolence, the breastplate of righteousness, the armor of truth, and just keep marching."

It was said that so devoted was his vast following that even among illiterates he could, by calm discussion of Platonic dogma, evoke deep cries of "Amen."

Dr. King also had a way of reducing complex issues to terms that anyone could understand. Thus, in the summer of 1965, when there was widespread discontent among Negroes about their struggle for equality of employment, he declared:

"What good does it do to be able to eat at a lunch counter if you can't buy a hamburger."

The enormous impact of Dr. King's words was one of the reasons he was in the President's Room in the Capitol on Aug. 6, 1965, when President Johnson signed the Voting Rights Act that struck down literacy tests, provided Federal registrars to assure the ballot to unregistered Negroes and marked the growth of the Negro as a political force in the South.

BACKED BY ORGANIZATION

Dr. King's effectiveness was enhanced and given continuity by the fact that he had an organization behind him. Formed in 1960, with headquarters in Atlanta, it was called the Southern Christian Leadership Conference, familiarly known as SLICK. Allied with it was another organization formed under Dr. King's sponsorship, the Student Nonviolent Coordinating Committee, often referred to as SNICK.

These two organizations reached the country, though their basic strength was in the South. They brought together Negro clergymen, businessmen, professional men and students. They raised the money and planned the sit-ins, the campaigns for Negro vote registration, the demonstrations by which Negroes hacked away at segregationist resistance, lowering the barriers against Negroes in the political, economic and social life of the nation.

This minister, who became the most famous spokesman for Negro rights since Booker T. Washington, was not particularly impressive in appearance. About 5 feet 8 inches tall, he had an oval face with almond-shaped eyes that looked almost dreamy when he was off the platform. His neck and shoulders were heavily muscled, but his hands were almost delicate.

SPEAKER OF FEW GESTURES

There was little of the rabblerouser in his oratory. He was not prone to extravagant gestures or loud peroration. His baritone voice, though vibrant, was not that of a spellbinder. Occasionally, after a particularly telling sentence, he would tilt his head a bit and fall silent as though waiting for the echoes of his thought to spread through the hall, church or street.

In private gatherings, Dr. King lacked the laughing gregariousness that often makes for popularity. Some thought he was without a sense of humor. He was not a gifted raconteur. He did not have the flamboyance of a Representative Adam Clayton Powell Jr. or the cool strategic brilliance of Roy Wilkins, head of the National Association for the Advancement of Colored People.

What Dr. King did have was an instinct for the right moment to make his moves. Some critics looked upon this as pure opportunism.

Nevertheless, it was this sense of timing that raised him in 1955, from a newly arrived minister in Montgomery, Ala., with his first church, to a figure of national prominence.

BUS BOYCOTT IN PROGRESS

Negroes in that city had begun a boycott of buses to win the right to sit where they pleased instead of being forced to move to the rear of buses, in Southern tradition or to surrender seats to white people when a bus was crowded.

The 381-day boycott by Negroes was already under way when the young pastor was placed in charge of the campaign. It has been said that one of the reasons he got the job was because he was so new in the area he had not antagonized any of the Negro factions. Even while the boycott was under way, a board of directors handled the bulk of administrative work.

However, it was Dr. King who dramatized the boycott with his decision to make it the testing ground, before the eyes of the nation, of his belief in the civil disobedience teachings of Thoreau and Gandhi. When he was arrested during the Montgomery boycott, he said:

"If we are arrested every day, if we are exploited every day, if we are trampled over every day, don't ever let anyone pull you so low as to hate them. We must use the weapon of love. We must have compassion and understanding for those who hate us. We must realize so many people are taught to hate us that they are not totally responsible for their hate. But we stand in life at midnight; we are always on the threshold of a new dawn."

HOME BOMBED IN ABSENCE

Even more dramatic, in some ways, was his reaction to the bombing of his home during the boycott. He was away at the time and rushed back fearful for his wife and children. They were not injured. But when he reached the modest house, more than a thousand Negroes had already gathered and were in an ugly mood, seeking revenge against the white people. The police were jittery. Quickly, Dr. King pacified the crowd and there was no trouble.

Dr. King was even more impressive during the "big push" in Birmingham, which began in April, 1963. With the minister in the limelight, Negroes there began a campaign of sit-ins at lunch counters, picketing and protest marches. Hundreds of children, used in the campaign, were jailed.

The entire world was stirred when the police turned dogs on the demonstrators. Dr. King was jailed for five days. While he was in prison he issued a 9,000-word letter that created considerable controversy among white people, alienating some sympathizers who thought Dr. King was being too aggressive.

MODERATES CALLED OBSTACLES

In the letter he wrote:

"I have almost reached the regrettable conclusion that the Negro's great stumbling block in the stride toward freedom is not the White Citizens Counciler or the Ku Klux Klanner, but the white moderate who is more devoted to order than to justice; who prefers a negative peace, which is the absence of tension, to a positive peace, which is the presence of justice."

Some critics of Dr. King said that one reason for this letter was to answer Negro intellectuals, such as the writer James Baldwin, who were impatient with Dr. King's belief in brotherhood. Whatever the reasons, the role of Dr. King in Birmingham added to his stature and showed that his enormous following was deeply devoted to him.

He demonstrated this in a threatening situation in Albany, Ga., after four Negro girls were killed in the bombing of a church. Dr. King said at the funeral:

"In spite of the darkness of this hour, we must not despair. We must not lose faith in our white brothers."

As Dr. King's words grew more potent and he was invited to the White House by Presidents Kennedy and Johnson, some critics —

Negroes as well as white — noted that sometimes, despite all the publicity he attracted, he left campaigns unfinished or else failed to attain his goals.

Dr. King was aware of this. But he pointed out, in 1964, in St. Augustine, Fla., one of the toughest civil rights battlegrounds, that there were important intangibles.

"Even if we do not get all we should," he said, "movements such as this tend more and more to give a Negro the sense of self-respect that he needs. It tends to generate courage in Negroes outside the movement. It brings intangible results outside the community where it is carried out. There is a hardening of attitudes in situations like this. But other cities see and say: 'We don't want to be another Albany or Birmingham,' and they make changes. Some communities, like this one, had to bear the cross."

It was in this city that Negroes marched into the fists of the mob singing: "We love everybody."

CONSCIOUS OF LEADING ROLE

There was no false modesty in Dr. King's self-appraisal of his role in the civil rights movement.

"History," he said, "has thrust me into this position. It would be both immoral and a sign of ingratitude if I did not face my moral responsibility to do what I can in this struggle."

Another time he compared himself to Socrates as one of "the creative gadflies of society."

At times he addressed himself deliberately to the white people of the nation. Once, he said:

"We will match your capacity to inflict suffering with our capacity to endure suffering. We will meet your physical force with soul force. We will not hate you, but we cannot in all good conscience obey your unjust laws … We will soon wear you down by our capacity to suffer. And in winning our freedom we will so appeal to your heart and conscience that we will win you in the process."

The enormous influence of Dr. King's voice in the turbulent racial conflict reached into New York in 1964. In the summer of that year racial rioting exploded in New York and in other Northern cities with large Negro populations. There was widespread fear that the disorders, particularly in Harlem, might set off unprecedented racial violence.

At this point Dr. King became one of the major intermediaries in restoring order. He conferred with Mayor Robert F. Wagner and with Negro leaders. A statement was issued, of which he was one of the signers, calling for "a broad curtailment if not total moratorium on mass demonstrations until after Presidential elections."

The following year, Dr. King was once more in the headlines and on television — this time leading a drive for Negro voter registration in Selma, Ala. Negroes were arrested by the hundreds. Dr. King was punched and kicked by a white man when, during this period of protest, he became the first Negro to register at a century-old hotel in Selma.

Martin Luther King Jr. was born Jan. 15, 1929, in Atlanta on Auburn Avenue. As a child his name was Michael Luther King and so was his father's. His father changed both their names legally to Martin Luther King in honor of the Protestant reformer.

Auburn Avenue is one of the nation's most widely known Negro sections. Many successful Negro business or professional men have lived there. The Rev. Martin Luther King Sr. was pastor of the Ebenezer Baptist Church at Jackson Street and Auburn Avenue.

Young Martin went to Atlanta's Morehouse College, a Negro institution whose students acquired what was sometimes called the "Morehouse swank." The president of Morehouse, Dr. B. E. Mays, took a special interest in Martin, who had decided, in his junior year, to be a clergyman.

He was ordained a minister in his father's church in 1947. It was in this church he was to say, some years later:

"America you've strayed away. You've trampled over 19 million of your brethren. All men are created equal. Not some men. Not white men. All men. America, rise up and come home."

Rev. Dr. Martin Luther King Jr.

Before Dr. King had his own church he pursued his studies in the integrated Crozier Theological Seminary, in Chester, Pa. He was one of six Negroes in a student body of about a hundred. He became the first Negro class president. He was named the outstanding student and won a fellowship to study for a doctorate at the school of his choice. The young man enrolled at Boston College in 1951.

For his doctoral thesis he sought to resolve the differences between the Harvard theologian Paul Tillich and the neonaturalist philosopher Henry Nelson Wieman. During this period he took courses at Harvard, as well.

While he was working on his doctorate he met Coretta Scott, a graduate of Antioch College, who was doing graduate work in music. He married the singer in 1953. They had four children, Yolanda, Martin Luther King 3d, Dexter Scott and Bernice.

In 1954, Dr. King became pastor of the Dexter Avenue Baptist Church in Montgomery, Ala. At that time few of Montgomery's white residents saw any reason for a major dispute with the city's 50,000 Negroes. They did not seem to realize how deeply the Negroes resented segregated seating on buses, for instance.

REVOLT BEGUN BY WOMAN

On Dec. 1, 1955, they learned, almost by accident. Mrs. Rosa Parks, a Negro seamstress, refused to comply with a bus driver's order to give up her seat to a white passenger. She was tired, she said. Her feet hurt from a day of shopping.

Mrs. Parks had been a local secretary for the National Association for the Advancement of Colored People. She was arrested, convicted of refusing to obey the bus conductor and fined $10 and costs, a total of $14. Almost as spontaneous as Mrs. Parks's act was the rallying of many Negro leaders in the city to help her.

From a protest begun over a Negro woman's tired feet Dr. King began his public career.

In 1959 Dr. King and his family moved back to Atlanta, where he became a co-pastor, with his father, of the Ebenezer Baptist Church.

As his fame increased, public interest in his beliefs led him to write books. It was while he was autographing one of these books, "Stride Toward Freedom," in a Harlem department store that he was stabbed by a Negro woman. It was in these books that he summarized, in detail, his beliefs as well as his career. Thus, in "Why We Can't Wait," he wrote:

"The Negro knows he is right. He has not organized for conquest or to gain spoils or to enslave those who have injured him. His goal is not to capture that which belongs to someone else. He merely wants, and will have, what is honorably his."

The possibility that he might someday be assassinated was considered by Dr. King on June 5, 1964, when he reported, in St. Augustine, Fla., that his life had been threatened. He said:

"Well, if physical death is the price that I must pay to free my white brothers and sisters from a permanent death of the spirit, then nothing can be more redemptive."

Plea by Mrs. King: 'Fulfill His Dream'

BY WALTER RUGABER | APRIL 7, 1968

ATLANTA, APRIL 6 — Mrs. Martin Luther King Jr. urged today that her slain husband's followers "join us in fulfilling his dream" of "a creative rather than a destructive way" out of the nation's racial problems.

Her plea, delivered in the sanctuary of the Ebenezer Baptist Church, which Dr. King had served as co-pastor, came as the violence and death sparked by her husband's assassination in Memphis Thursday raged through a number of the nation's major cities.

"He gave his life for the poor of the world — the garbage workers of Memphis and the peasants of Vietnam," Mrs. King said. Dr. King had gone to Memphis to organize a march in support of the city's striking sanitation employees.

"Nothing hurt him more than that man could attempt no way to solve problems except through violence," the widow continued. "He gave his life in search of a more excellent way, a more effective way, a creative rather than a destructive way."

Mrs. King, wearing a black dress and speaking in a clear and steady voice, said at a news conference that "we intend to go on in search of that way, and I hope that you who loved and admired him would join us in fulfilling his dream."

Services for Dr. King are scheduled to begin at 10:30 A.M. Tuesday with brief worship at the Ebenezer Church, where Dr. King had served with his father, the Rev. Dr. Martin Luther King Sr.

Then the mourners are to march through the city to Morehouse College, the predominantly Negro institution that Dr. King attended as an undergraduate. A longer service, set for 1 P.M., will be outdoors in the quadrangle there.

The church has a limited seating capacity. However, the Rev. Rev. Ralph D. Abernathy said the quadrangle, together with adjoining areas of the campus that will be connected by a public address system, could accommodate as many as 100,000 persons.

Mr. Abernathy, who succeeded Dr. King as president of the Southern Christian Leadership Conference, appeared before the newsmen with Mrs. King.

The slain leader's wife asked that "friends, supporters, and well-wishers," instead of sending flowers, send funds for the continuation of Dr. King's work to the leadership conference at 334 Auburn Avenue, N.E., Atlanta, Ga., 30303.

HUNDREDS FILE PAST

Today, hundreds of mourners gathered to file past Dr. King's body, scheduled to lie in state until 4 P.M. Monday at Sister's Chapel on the campus of Spelman College, a girl's school near Morehouse.

The throngs began filing past the open coffin shortly after 6:30 P.M. They were delayed for about an hour while Mrs. King, accompanied by several members of the family and friends, entered the chapel privately.

With the widow were Dr. King's brother, the Rev. A. D. Williams King; his sister, Mrs. Christine Farris; his mother, Mrs. Martin Luther King Sr.; his secretary, Miss Dora McDonald, and Harry Belafonte, the singer.

The coffin in which the body returned from Memphis yesterday has been exchanged for one of mahogany. The new coffin rested on a portable stand, with about two dozen floral arrangements nearly. Dr. King was dressed in a black suit and a white shirt.

EXECUTIVES AND DOMESTICS

The mourners, who ranged from business men dressed in conservative suits to domestic workers wearing aprons, often displayed emotion. One woman fainted, and a second nearly did so as she passed the coffin.

Some snapped pictures, but the crowd was orderly and obeyed when ushers urged them to move on. Several of Dr. King's aides stood by in the chapel, where an organist played solemn music.

There was a scattering of whites among those waiting. No trouble was reported. On Monday, the body will be brought to the church to lie in state there until the funeral begins at 10:30 A.M.

Mr. Abernathy said that anger and bitterness among Negroes were understandable, but he said that "Dr. King was not a man of violence [and] it is my hope that we will not burn these cities down."

APPEARS AT CHURCH

Mrs. King had been invited to make her statement at a local television studio to permit a live national broadcast. But she refused to appear except at the Ebenezer Baptist Church. Technical difficulties prevented live telecasting there.

An informed source said it was first thought that Dr. King's father might make the statement, a stronger and more direct plea for nonviolence was drafted for him last night before Mrs. King decided to make her remarks.

Mrs. King did not refer directly to racial violence in the nation during her 11-minute appearance before newspaper reporters and television cameramen this afternoon. She left the church immediately after making the statement.

Mrs. King sat at a narrow wooden table before the pulpit. Behind her, high on a wall of the church, was a stained glass window depicting a praying Christ. Cameras clicked constantly as she spoke.

Blinking into the bright lights, the widow said she would have preferred to be alone with her children. She said that "the response from so many friends around the world has been very comforting to us.

"He knew that at any moment his physical life could be cut short," Mrs. King said, "and we faced this squarely and honestly. My husband faced the possibility of death without bitterness or hatred."

She continued:

"He knew that this was a sick society, totally infested with racism and violence that questioned his integrity, maligned his motives, and distorted his views, and he struggled with every ounce of his energy to save that society from itself.

"He never hated, he never despaired of well-doing, and he encouraged us to do likewise. I am surprised and pleased at the success of his teaching, for our children say calmly, 'Daddy is not dead. He may be physically dead, but his spirit will never die.' "

Rights Leader's Undaunted Widow

BY THE NEW YORK TIMES | APRIL 9, 1968

WHEN MRS. MARTIN LUTHER KING JR. announced that she would interrupt her mourning for her husband and take his place at the head of a civil rights march yesterday in Memphis, a sorrowing world heralded the widow's strength. But to her friends and her husband's associates, Coretta Scott King's strength has never been surprising. It has been lending quiet support and a calming spirit to the Southern Christian Leadership Conference since its founding by Dr. King.

Mrs. King is a small woman with honeybrown skin and loose dark hair. Her voice is soft, her manner dignified. She is always neat and when she marched by her husband's side at the head of the civil rights demonstration in Selma, Aka., in 1965, friends said that it was the first they had seen her in public in flat-heeled shoes.

She made a number of public appearances on behalf of the civil rights movement, often at her husband's side, but also by herself.

SPEAKS TO 50,000

In April of 1967 she addressed a crowd of 50,000 in San Francisco for the Spring Mobilization to End the War in Vietnam while her husband was addressing a joint demonstration in New York.

She developed a concert that she took to cities around the country for the benefit of the Southern Christian Leadership Conference.

The concerts, which raised more than $55,000, combined a lecture, poetry and music that told the history of the civil rights movement. Mrs. King narrated and sang.

She studied voice and piano at Lincoln High School in Marion, Ala., where she was born on April 27, 1927, and majored in music at Antioch College in Yellow Springs, Ohio. She went on to study at the New England Conservatory of Music in Boston.

A quiet strength characterizes all her activities. (Dr. and Mrs. King with New York City Mayor Robert F. Wagner during a presentation of the city's Medallion of Honor in 1964.)

She made her concert debut at the Second Baptist Church in Springfield and later gave concerts in cities throughout the United States.

On a trip to India in 1959 with Dr. King she sang Negro spirituals at the Gandharva Mahavidyalaya Music School in New Delhi and received a good review from the music critic of The Times of India.

Mrs. King has received numerous honors, including the brotherhood award of the National Council of Negro Women in 1957 and an award from the American Jewish Congress for her work in the area of peace and human relations.

In 1960 she was a delegate-at-large to the White House Conference on Children and Youth.

She was a member of the Women's Strike for Peace who went to the 17-nation Disarmament Conference in Geneva in 1962. In 1966 her name was on the Gallup Poll of most admired women.

Mrs. King has been raising her children — Yolanda Denise, now 12 years old; Martin Luther King 3d, 10; Dexter Scott, 7, and Bernice Albertine, 5 — with the same quiet strength that has characterized all her activities.

After her marriage to Dr. King on June 18, 1953, Mrs. King spent many hours visiting him in various jails where he served sentences for nonviolent demonstrations for Negro equality.

She used to tell the children:

"Daddy's gone to jail to help the people. They don't have good homes to live in. They don't have enough food. Daddy would like all the people to have these things."

In a lecture in Seattle in 1965 she said:

"You realize that what you are doing is pretty dangerous, but we go on with the faith that what we are doing is right. If something happens to my husband, the cause will continue. It may even be helped."

Mrs. King to Speak at Anti-Vietnam War Rally

BY THE NEW YORK TIMES | APRIL 19, 1968

MRS. MARTIN LUTHER KING JR. has agreed to speak in her husband's place at the anti-Vietnam War rally to be held in Central Park on April 27. Before he was slain in Memphis on April 4, Dr. King had been listed as the rally's keynote speaker.

The sponsors, the Fifth Avenue Vietnam Peace Parade Committee, hope that the rally in the park and five marches that will feed it will generate an outpouring of 100,000 people opposed to the war.

Mrs. King's agreement to speak at the rally was announced here yesterday by the parade committee and confirmed in Atlanta at the headquarters of the Southern Christian Leadership Conference, the civil rights and peace organization founded by Dr. King.

David Dellinger, coordinator of the parade committee, said: "Coretta King is coming to speak because she is concerned that since his death her husband is being remembered by many people only for his civil rights activities. She is anxious to re-establish his role in people's minds as an antiwar leader."

LINDSAY ALSO TO SPEAK

Among others who have agreed to speak at the rally are Mayor Lindsay, Dick Gregory, night club performer; Viveca Lindfors, the actress; the Rev. William Sloan Coffin of Yale University, Rabbi Maurice Eisendrath of the Union of American Hebrew Congregations, Stanley Wise of the Student Non-Violent Coordinating Committee, David Livingston of District 65, Retail, Wholesale and Department Store Workers Union, and Greg Bradford, a Marine Corps veteran of the Vietnam War.

The committee said that Senators Robert F. Kennedy and Eugene McCarthy had been invited to speak, but had declined because they were busy with their primary campaigns.

The two principal feeder marches will be down Fifth Avenue from 95th Street and down Central Park West from 107th Street. Others will start at Third Avenue and 125th Street, Lenox Avenue and 145th Street and at the Manhattan end of the Queensborough Bridge.

A sixth march that would start in Washington Square Park is being discussed by Youth Against War and Fascism and the United States Committee to Aid the National Liberation Front.

April 27 also is the date of the annual Loyalty Day Parade, which this year will move up Fifth Avenue from 36th to 52d Streets.

TV: Mrs. King Takes March Spotlight

BY JACK GOULD | JUNE 20, 1968

LIVE TELEVISION COVERAGE of the "Solidarity Day" ceremonies of the Poor People's campaign in Washington was extremely limited and perhaps not without reasonable journalistic justification. In comparison with the memorable 1963 Washington march, in which the Rev. Dr. Martin Luther King Jr. gave voice to his dreams, the crowd was small and the element of inspiration not present in like degree.

But thanks to the habit of the National Broadcasting Company news department, which does not believe in prejudging what may be the running time of a spot news event, there was a significant development of genuine interest. Mrs. Coretta King, Dr. King's widow, easily emerged as the most arresting leader on TV of the cause of Negro liberation and the alleviation of the economically depressed. The presence of a woman champion of equality for all races, adhering tastefully to the views of her assassinated husband, was something new and touching.

Mrs. King's versatility and dedication were undeniably distinctive. She set aside her own career in music to raise a family, but yesterday before the Lincoln Memorial she sang "Come by Here, My Lord." She also movingly read a poem by the late Langston Hughes on a Negro mother's commitment to urge her son to climb upward despite all interim frustrations and setbacks over which he has no control.

But in television terms there was an echo of Dr. King's oratory in Mrs. King's appeal for the mobilization of woman power, regardless of color, to move to the forefront in combating racism, poverty and the killing in Vietnam. Hers was an appeal to those who bear the children facing the future's uncertainties and, as fully reported by N.B.C., was altogether arresting.

The American Broadcasting Company scheduled its half-hour special at 4 P.M., so it missed what appeared to be the day's dramatic

Coretta Scott King addressing the "Solidarity Day" rally yesterday.

climax, and the Columbia Broadcasting System quickly cut away from Mrs. King after she had finished singing. The N.B.C. news department obviously has the leeway and sensitivity to make certain that life is not always quite so predictable.

In the response of the crowd in Washington, the camera caught the importance of Mrs. King's decision to carry on her husband's work. In contrast to other speeches by white and Negro men involved in the black cause, Mrs. King was easily the major figure of an occasion inevitably invoking remembrances of past national tragedies.

In the late afternoon TV accounts, supplemented by excerpts in regular newscasts, the problem of the Negro community in finding a new leader to replace Dr. King was manifest. From accounts on the home screen it was suggested that the number of white persons participating in "Solidarity Day" actually outnumbered blacks, but the cameras were remiss in showing the home audience whether this was or was not the case.

C.B.S. captured one fascinating sequence in which the assembled throng thoroughly cheered Senator Eugene J. McCarthy and gave only mixed courtesy applause with outright boos for Vice President Humphrey, a political development duly noted but not significantly expanded upon.

How M.L.K.'s Death Helped Lead to Gun Control in the U.S.

BY RICHARD A. OPPEL JR. | APRIL 3, 2018

THE 1960S WERE KNOWN for their turmoil, but the degree to which guns were a factor is sometimes overlooked. Not only was a president assassinated, but an ex-Marine opened fire from an observation deck in Austin and the homicide rate leaped by more than 50 percent, driven by fatal shootings. Gun sales soared, prompted by fears of violence and rioting.

But the mayhem and violence didn't seem to move a Congress that refused to take gun-control legislation seriously. It would not even approve a proposal to outlaw the mail-order purchase of rifles, like the one Lee Harvey Oswald bought for $19.95, plus shipping and handling, and used to kill President Kennedy.

One of the few major gun control measures enacted, in California, was a reaction not to violence but to the Black Panthers' exercising their right to bear arms by patrolling with loaded rifles.

The political calculus began to change on April 4, 1968. The Rev. Dr. Martin Luther King Jr. was gunned down in Memphis. Nine weeks later, Senator Robert F. Kennedy was fatally shot in Los Angeles.

Finally, gun control became a possibility — at least in the hands of President Lyndon B. Johnson, a master at turning tragedy into legislative gain. He had used the death of President John F. Kennedy to pass the Civil Rights Act, and wrung the Voting Rights Act from the Bloody Sunday march from Selma to Montgomery. Now he would try for the Gun Control Act.

Today, it's not clear that any shooting could be awful enough to embolden Congress to thwart the National Rifle Association. But even back then, the N.R.A. throttled much of what Mr. Johnson intended to do.

"The voices that blocked these safeguards were not the voices of an aroused nation," an angry president said at the bill signing. "They were the voices of a powerful lobby, a gun lobby, that has prevailed for the moment in an election year."

He called on "those of us who are really concerned about crime" to fight for stronger laws. "We have been through a great deal of anguish these last few months and these last few years — too much anguish to forget so quickly."

The new law outlawed gun sales to felons, drug abusers, minors and those with mental illness; banned most out-of-state and mail-order gun sales; and sharply curbed imported weapons, including the cheap, tiny pistols used in many homicides.

It remains a cornerstone of federal gun law today.

The King assassination spurred the legislation not just because it horrified the nation, but also because it prompted unrest across the country, including in Washington, where lawmakers watched rioters come within blocks of the White House as thousands of federal troops were mobilized.

"It was in Congress's backyard, so they didn't have to read about it in the newspapers. They could see it," said Larry Temple, a high-ranking aide and special counsel to Mr. Johnson. "The death of Dr. King and the resulting riots in Washington had an impact on Congress and what they wound up doing."

But it wasn't until June 5, when Senator Kennedy was assassinated, that the logjam looked like it would break. A day later, a modest gun-control proposal that had languished passed Congress, raising the age to buy handguns to 21.

Still, Mr. Johnson wanted something far more sweeping. He proposed to treat guns like cars: They would be registered and their owners would be licensed.

Had something like this passed, gun-control proponents say, the United States today might look more like Britain or Australia, countries where guns are tracked and gun violence is a fraction of what it is here.

"He said, 'We have about 10 days or two weeks to get it passed,' " recalled Joseph Califano, his chief domestic adviser. " 'If we don't get it out of committee by then, the N.R.A. will kill us.' "

This time, there has been no similar urgency in Washington, even as hundreds of thousands of protesters in the capital and elsewhere have demanded changes after the killing of 17 students and staff at a high school in Parkland, Fla.

Crime is less a concern, as the murder rate has fallen sharply since the sixties. But mass shootings have become frighteningly common. Anyone — or anyone's child — could be a victim, at a school, a concert, a church, a movie theater or a nightclub.

And while a smaller percent of households own guns, the country has more of them, and they are deadlier: Semiautomatic rifles like the AR-15 have become the weapon of choice in the largest recent mass killings, leading to death tolls in the dozens.

Most people today favor tighter gun restrictions, polls indicate, just as they did a half-century ago. But the N.R.A. also wields political power disproportionate to the size of its membership, as it did then.

In 1968, the organization was not yet as uncompromising as it is today. But it used tactics that would feel familiar now.

It flooded its members with sky-is-falling warnings about the government taking away gun rights, and urged them to hound lawmakers. In a letter to 900,000 N.R.A. members in June 1968, the organization's president, Harold W. Glassen, said that the "right of sportsmen" to lawfully own and use firearms was "in the greatest jeopardy in the history of our country."

Frustrated gun-control backers called it "calculated hysteria and distortion." But it was profoundly effective.

In its coverage that month, The New York Times called the gun lobby among the most effective in Washington, citing the association's ability to get "sportsmen, farmers and gun lovers to put pressure on their congressmen."

Soon, Mr. Johnson's favored provisions were shorn from the bill by his old cadre of fellow Southern Democrats.

"Strom Thurmond is hostile as hell, and so is Jim," — James O. Eastland, Democrat of Mississippi — "and they're mutilating the bill as it is," the leader of the Senate Republicans, Everett Dirksen of Illinois, told Mr. Johnson in a recorded phone call on July 24, 1968, that is in Mr. Johnson's presidential library. (Senator Thurmond was by then a Republican.)

The licensing and registration provisions passed neither chamber, and triumphant pro-gun forces announced it was now legislation they could "live with."

To which Representative Charles S. Joelson, Democrat of New Jersey, responded: "I suggest that tens of thousands of Americans can die with it."

The Gun Control Act was signed into law that fall.

Two years later, the N.R.A. helped defeat the re-election bid of a leading Senate proponent of tough gun laws, Joseph D. Tydings, Democrat of Maryland, a man who had won his seat just six years earlier in a landslide.

By now the N.R.A. has perfected the art of going after lawmakers who defy the organization. That is one reason the demands of mass shooting survivors and their allies, now led most visibly by the Parkland students, remain so far apart from the measures Congress is considering.

In 1956, after his house was bombed, Dr. King applied to the local sheriff for a permit to carry a concealed handgun. He was denied on the grounds that he was "unsuitable," according to Adam Winkler, the author of "Gunfight: The Battle Over the Right to Bear Arms in America."

Friends and relatives who feared for his safety urged him to hire a bodyguard and armed watchmen, he wrote in his autobiography. But soon, he and Coretta Scott King, his wife, reconsidered and gave up the one gun they owned. "How could I serve as one of the leaders of a nonviolent movement and at the same time use weapons of violence for my personal protection?" he wrote.

Fifty years ago, the death of great leaders prodded Congress to act on gun control. Now, at a similar juncture, it is the death of schoolchildren that has stirred the makings of a movement. It remains uncertain whether the current movement for gun restrictions will result in meaningful reform.

So far, the main impetus is in state legislatures. "Even in Republican-controlled states it appears there is at least some openness to doing something, building on the foundation laid over the last five years in less conservative states," said Adam Skaggs, chief counsel of the Giffords Law Center to Prevent Gun Violence. But he said Congress may not do much unless midterm elections shake things up.

For Dr. King, who would have turned 89 in January, getting rid of his gun helped him reckon with his mortality and focus on his movement.

"From that point on, I no longer needed a gun nor have I been afraid," he wrote. "Had we become distracted by the question of my safety we would have lost the moral offensive and sunk to the level of our oppressors."

Malcolm X

Unlike other prominent civil rights activists, Malcolm X — known later as El-Hajj Malik El-Shabazz — took a volatile, no-holds-barred approach to racial inequality. He was charismatic and well-spoken, and as a leading member of the Black Muslims he became a powerful public figure known for his black nationalist views. As time passed, he became conflicted and broke from the Black Muslims, but was shot and killed by several of its members on February 21, 1965. Yet his ideas and goals linger on even after his death, resonating with later generations who are eager to speak out against injustice.

Negroes Say Conditions in U.S. Explain Nationalists' Militancy

BY ROBERT L. TEAGUE | MARCH 2, 1961

Following is the second of two articles on extremist groups seeking to rouse American Negroes to a more militant attitude in their efforts to obtain equality.

"MERE CRUMBS FROM the tables of an abundant society have made millions of black men angry. That's why there was a riot at the U. N. the other day, and why the black nationalist movement is growing and becoming more militant in New York and everywhere else."

These are the words of James Lawson, president of the United African Nationalist Movement, who was one of forty-three persons interviewed last week on black nationalism.

The forty-three, nearly all Harlem Negroes, echoed Mr. Lawson's analysis again and again. But as to specific goals and the way to seek them, there is a diversity of opinion. However, none advocated violence, "except in self-defense."

As an example of how far the opinions range, the Black Muslims are opposed to integration. They say they will settle for nothing less than a separate sovereign state.

The Muslim aims were described by the leader of Temple of Islam No. 7 on 116th Street. He is called Minister Malcolm X.

At a Lenox Avenue restaurant, one of several businesses owned and operated by Muslims, Minister Malcolm explained the "X." He said: "All who follow Mr. [Elijah] Muhammad have given their slave names back to the white man. We've also given him back his whisky, his dope, his politics and all his other vices. And we reject his blue-eyed God. Islam is the natural religion of black mankind." Elijah Muhammad is the group's national leader.

Minister Malcolm is a lean, energetic six-footer, about 35 years old. He has sandy hair, and a fair complexion and wears horn-rimmed glasses and a scholarly mien.

Minister Malcolm said that in "begging for integration" for years, the Negro had barely attracted the white man's attention. "But we've shaken up the white man by asking for separation," he said. "To beg the white man to let you eat in his restaurant feeds his ego. But we feel that the black man's 310 years of labor is worth more than a cup o' coffee in a white cafe or a house in a cracker neighborhood. We are here to collect back wages."

Minister Malcolm said his group wanted a land grant from the Federal Government and gold to help build a separate state "somewhere along the seaboard."

CRITICS ARE CRITICIZED

In commenting on Negroes who denounce the black nationalist movement, Minister Malcolm said: "Those are Black Pharisees, middle-class Negroes satisfied with things as they are so long as they are permitted to be comfortable and live out their lives as carbon copies of the white man."

Minister Malcolm readily admitted that he was an ex-convict. "A lot of our people are ex-Christians, ex-dope addicts, ex-bums and ex-Negroes," he said. "And a lot have been upper-class citizens all their lives. The white man likes to think that only the riffraff, the unemployed and the ignorant are in our organization. But I don't think any white group in the country has more intelligent people than we."

He charged that there had been false reports that the Muslims had participated in the outburst at the United Nations in which more than two dozen persons were injured.

Cultists on Coast Denounce Police

BY BILL BECKER | MAY 6, 1962

Negroes charge brutality in death — 9 accused in fray.

LOS ANGELES, MAY 5 — Charges of violence and brutality were exchanged between Los Angeles officials and Negro leaders after the death this week of a moslem Negro Muslim cultist.

A grand jury investigation was set for May 15. Meanwhile, nine members of the Muslim cult were arraigned on criminal charges of assault with intent to commit bodily harm.

Six wounded Muslims, awaiting arraignment, were recovering in Los Angeles General Hospital.

Ronald T. Stokes, 29 years old, secretary of Los Angeles Mosque Number 27, was killed in the affray between the police and cultists April 28. One policeman was wounded and two others were severely beaten.

William H. Parker, chief of police, told a preliminary grand jury committee that the Muslims were "a hate organization dedicated to the destruction of the Caucasian race."

MEMBERSHIP ESTIMATED

Chief Parker placed the membership of the group here at 2,000 to 3,000. Nationally, the sect is believed to have 60,000 members.

"Their teachings are of the nature that such clashes are bound to recur and will become more frequent," the police chief said. He said the Muslims had a trained "muscle squad" called the F. O. I., or Fruits of Islam, and added:

"I feel this sect should be exposed like any threat to the community."

The Muslims countered by holding a news conference at which Malcolm X., also known as Malik Shabazz, Minister of Mosque No. 7, 102 West 116th Street, New York City, denied Muslims were anti-white. He accused Chief Parker of Gestapo tactics and false propaganda.

Articulate and smartly dressed in a brown suit (most cultists wear black), Mr. X gave other information but declined to give his full American name. He is 36 years old, was born in Omaha, Neb., and is a disciple of Elijah Muhammed, Chicago leader of the cult.

MOVEMENT OPPOSED

The movement has been denounced by the National Association for the Advancement of Colored People and other Negro groups favoring integration. But the N. A. A. C. P. asked both Attorney General Robert F. Kennedy and Stanley Mosk, California Attorney General, to conduct investigations.

Mayor Samuel W. Yorty joined Chief Parker in describing the Muslims as "an extremely dangerous group." He said he would like "to have the Muslims dealt with through the many fine leaders in our Negro community."

The sect here, as in most cities of the United States, appears to be a small minority of the Negro population. There are about 300,000 Negroes in the Los Angeles population of 2,700,000.

But the local branch of the N. A. A. C. P. protested "the unnecessary killing" and "brutality."

In its telegram to Attorney General Mosk, the N. A. A. C. P. said its information indicated "the full facts have not been presented and a deliberate attempt has been made to inflame public opinion."

Chief Parker has been accused before by minority groups of callousness toward Negroes and Mexican-Americans.

"Evidence in this case shows inefficiency by police and utter disregard for civil rights," Dr. H. Claude Hudson, a member of the national board of the N. A. A. C. P., said.

Mr. X, or Malcolm, as he prefers, said Muslims believed in "separation."

"Separation is the division of two equals," he said.

He said members of the cult followed the tenets of Islam, the Mohammedan faith, because they thought that it was the basic religion of Africa, whence they sprang. He said members did not drink, smoke or carry weapons.

Mr. X said that Muslims had achieved respect from the New York City police. "We want to clean up our own people," he said.

"We eliminate drunkenness, drug addiction, juvenile delinquency, fornication and adultery."

CHARGES 'BRUTAL CRIME'

Mr. X described the shooting as "police-state murder" and a "brutal crime against innocent unarmed human beings."

He charged that a squad of seventy-five officers shot or clubbed sixteen Muslim members during the affray. The wounded were denied medical treatment for hours, he contended. He also said bullets had been found on the floor of the Muslim temple on South Broadway in the heart of the Negro district.

The riot began, the police said, when two patrolmen halted a car with a load of clothes just outside the temple. Two men in the car lunged at them, the policemen said. Then others ran out of the temple to join the fight.

The men in the car were employees of a cleaning company and both were unarmed, Mr. X said. He added that the trouble had begun when an officer twisted an arm of one of the men.

Assertive Spirit Stirs Negroes, Puts Vigor in Civil Rights Drive

BY M. S. HANDLER | APRIL 23, 1963

Racial pride increases throughout U.S. — 'Black Nationalism' is viewed as a powerful force for change.

A NEW ASSERTIVE MOOD, characterized by some Negro leaders as "Black Nationalism," is spreading throughout the United States.

This spirit is usually identified by the general public with the Black Muslims, the extremist group dedicated to the establishment of a Negro nation carved out of America.

But, in the opinion of many responsible Negro observers, this new mood also lies behind movements with much greater Negro support — the voter registration drive in Greenwood, Miss., and the assault by the Rev. Dr. Martin Luther King Jr. on segregation in Birmingham, Ala., to cite two examples.

For the term Black Nationalism is now used by Negroes to embrace a multitude of feelings, many of them contradictory, but all having one concept in common — identification of America's Negro population as a group with a common heritage of suffering and achievement, engaged in mass action to compel the white majority to recognize and implement their legal rights.

A WAY OF LIFE

A Negro social philosopher, Dr. C. Eric Lincoln of Clark College in Atlanta, explains that Black Nationalism developed because "the Negro is required to be Negro before, and sometimes to the exclusion of, anything else."

But Dr. Lincoln says that this new mood goes beyond earlier appeals for equality.

"Black Nationalism is more than courage and rebellion," he says,

Malcolm X speaking at an outdoor rally.

"It is a way of life," rejecting white symbols and culture and emphasizing pride in being black.

As yet Black Nationalism has not developed into an organized political force, although the potentiality worries both Republicans and Democrats.

DEMOCRAT TAKES NOTE

Louis Martin, a Negro, who is deputy chairman of the Democratic National Committee, notes the rising demands of his race to improve its lot and says Negro aspirations can be summed up in one phrase:

"White man, move over."

Negro leaders differ in their assessment of this new mood, but they agree that it is a powerful new force in American public life.

It is threatening the old order of Negro leaders, the business and professional class and ministers. It is questioning the co-leadership of liberal whites in the struggle against discrimination.

Moreover, it is helping destroy the stereotypes of the shiftless Negro as well as the Uncle Toms.

HEARTACHES FOR SOME

It is bringing new heartaches as Negro parents find they no longer understand their children, who are filled with new racial pride. It has also brought to the surface wide-spread hatred for the white man.

One highly placed Negro leader, who has dedicated his life to integration within the present framework of society, sadly remarked:

"There is a bit of hatred in every Negro's heart. The Negro would not be human if he did not resent the oppression to which he has been subjected. But this feeling would be stifled if the Negro were to receive the equal status he is entitled to as a citizen of this country."

Black Nationalism as a mood is to be found in varying degrees in all segments of the Negro population, but only the Black Muslims expound a complete renunciation of coexistence with the whites.

Malcolm X, the dynamic leader of the Black Muslims in New York, contends that the Negroes "have already seceded" emotionally and intellectually from American society.

To this, Roy Wilkins, the executive secretary of the National Association for the Advancement of Colored People replies:

"Hogwash. Ninety-nine per cent of the Negroes want in."

In an interview published this week in U. S. News & World Report, Mr. Wilkins described the dominant mood of the Negroes today as "very great impatience" with the slow progress toward the "status of full citizenship." He said the Black Muslims are an outgrowth of this sentiment. But he pointed out that for the Muslims, "idea of black for black has always been around in one form or another."

However, even the most bitter opponent of the Black Muslims agrees that they have contributed to the growth in Negro racial pride, group identification, self-respect and the conscious worth of Negro values.

The Black Muslims have never published any figures about their membership, but estimates have ranged from as low as 25,000 to as high as 250,000, with the number often put as 70,000. None of these estimates, however, is based on verifiable data. There are more than 18,000,000 Negroes in the country.

FOLLOWERS OF ISLAM

The Muslims assert that they are faithful followers of Islam, a claim that raises some doubts among their opponents. The Muslims, note, however, that Elijah Muhammed, head of the movement, has made a pilgrimage to Mecca, a journey reserved for Islam's faithful.

The Black Muslims reject Christianity as a white man's religion imposed on the Negroes to insure their prolonged servitude and inferior status. Christianity promises rewards in the hereafter, and according to the Black Muslims, this belief is designed to condition Negroes to accept their inferior status on this earth. But all the old-line Negro leaders insist that the Christian churches are the most powerful force in the Negro community, without which no gains can be made.

The Black Muslims are organized in a vertical chain of command that makes for authoritarian control vested in Elijah Muhammed, who resides in Chicago. A highly trained praetorian guard, called Fruit of Islam, assures almost military discipline and unquestioning execution of orders.

This elite was recruited in part in penitentiaries among prisoners who were later rehabilitated.

Malcolm X, who is of impressive bearing and is endowed with a shrewd mind, today overshadows Elijah Muhammed.

RISING POPULARITY

Other Negro leaders are very conscious of the growing popularity of Malcolm X. While they reject his contention that alienation of the Negroes from the American social order is "an accomplished fact," they concede that he is able.

They also grudgingly agree that the puritanical code of the move-ment — its prohibition of smoking, drinking, gambling, prostitution and narcotics, is destroying the old symbols affixed to Negroes.

The obscure origins of the Black Muslims used to generate deri-sion. But one visit to the Black Muslim restaurant on Lenox Avenue is enough to silence those who make fun of the movement. Waiters dressed in immaculate white jackets and black trousers move about quietly. Mirrors glisten and tables, chairs and floor are almost anti-septically clean.

The old-line leaders also note that Black Muslim ideology, which preaches racial pride, is sweeping Negro communities.

For example, a distinguished Negro who is committed to a "social contract" between the white and Negro populations tells the story of his daughter, the only Negro pupil in an upper middle class school in Westchester County. Though friendly and helpful at school, white pupils refused to attend her Christmas party. She was deeply hurt but said nothing. Several months later, without the knowledge of her parents she wrote a moving essay for school on the meaning of being black.

WARNS OF DANGERS

James Farmer, executive secretary of the Congress of Racial Equality warns of the perils of Black Nationalism. CORE is the organization identified with the sit-ins, freedom rides and voters' registration.

"There is the possibility that Black Nationalism could develop into hate of everything that is different," he says. "How it turns out will depend on how successful the Negroes will be in bringing down the barriers to desegregation."

Whitney Moore Young Jr., executive director of the National Urban League, which has contributed greatly to equal job opportunity, assessed the situation even more seriously.

"In previous generations the Negro believed what is white is right," he said. "This was the standard to which the Negro aspired. This has changed. The Negro is taking a second look and is rejecting many of the white man's values and codes of behavior."

Mr. Young attributed the radical change in the Negro's attitude to the fact that "he no longer feels innately inferior to the white man."

This point was brought home to a white man who drove a few blocks out of his way to take a Negro home. As the Negro got out of the car, he turned and said:

"Thanks for the lift. It was mighty black of you."

NEGROES ARE DIVIDED

There seems to be a sharp cleavage between Negro intellectuals and Negro organization officials in their assessment of the Negro's viewpoint. The intellectuals are closer to James Baldwin, the Negro author, sharing his anger, despair and rage.

In his essay, "Letter From A Region In My Mind," Mr. Baldwin, said:

"The treatment accorded the Negro during the Second World War marks, for me, a turning point in the Negro's relation to America. To put it briefly, and somewhat too simply, a certain hope died, a certain respect for white Americans faded. One began to pity them, or to hate them."

Many New York City Negro intellectuals are categorical in their belief that the Negro fundamentally hates the white man.

They insist that this hatred is spreading as the entrenched white men in the North resort to more refined and resourceful techniques of confining the Negroes to black ghettos, denying them equal work opportunities and hospital facilities and arranging de facto school segregation and token desegregation of the major institutions of higher learning.

Dr. Kenneth Clark, Negro professor of psychology at the City College of New York, says "the Negro does not feel himself a part of this white dominated country, and there is no reason why he should concern himself with this country's international relations."

"There is a colossal indifference to the United States Government's foreign problems," he said. "If I were to talk to a Negro crowd about foreign affairs people would say to me, 'man, what are you talking about?' "

Mr. Farmer says this lack of interest is due more to Negroes' preoccupation with their own problems than to a conscious withdrawal from the problems of the United States.

Thus students at the all-Negro Atlanta University said they were not interested in and did not favor the American Government's Cuban policy until last fall when war seemed near.

Asked why they changed their minds, one replied: "Well we wanted to find out why we might have to get killed."

WIDENING GULF

The evidence seems to indicate that the widening gulf between the dominant white majority and the Negro minority in the United States is paralleled by a growing gulf separating the educated Negroes from the Negroes masses.

For example, Atlanta University students from rural districts said they had lost contact with their own families after a brief time at the university. They said they found it difficult to communicate when they returned home during the holidays.

Such alienation is found in all societies, but it apparently is more acute for the Negro because of his struggle for civil rights. Professor Samuel duBois Cook, Negro sociologist of Atlanta University, explains the effect of education on Negroes:

"In a sense the Negro's very progress tends to magnify his frustrations, insecurities, anxieties, tensions and pathetic dilemmas. For his unsatisfied desires expand, his longings intensify, his expectations are greater, his level of aspiration soars, and his imagination and vision are more lucid, inspired and vivid. Accordingly, his disappointments are more bitter, roadblocks more intolerable, barriers more baffling and gnawing, suffering more poignant. Success aggravates failure. Failure erodes success."

Southern students publicly accept Dr. King's approach of non-violence as the guideline for all assaults on segregation.

Nevertheless, they seem attracted to the extremist view of Malcolm X, although reluctant to discuss them.

Leslie Dunbar, of the Southern Regional Council, one of the white men most intimately associated with Negro communities in the South, says it is difficult, if not impossible, to ascertain the true feelings and aspirations of the Negroes. He doubts whether the Negro leaders themselves are fully cognizant of what the Negro masses want because, he says, the Negro almost instinctively hides his feelings, even from members of his own race. Malcolm X goes even further:

"Because of his special history the Negro has had to become a two-faced individual. I could take you to a round of meetings in one evening and you would find the same Negroes responding enthusiastically to the most divergent point of view on the same theme. And this is when he is among his own people."

But Malcolm X believes he knows where the Negro masses stand:

"The black masses in this country are not divided, it is the leadership that is divided.

"The established Negro leaders have lulled the white man into believing everything is under control. There is a difference of night and day when a white man and a Negro say 'our country.' The white man means it. The Negro behaves like a house dog and wags his tail."

Malcolm X maintains that the Negroes should dispense with white liberal leadership and guidance in the civil rights fight. This view, which is shared in part by moderate Negroes, is based on two assumptions.

The first is that the Negroes have developed enough leaders capable of taking charge of their own struggle. The second is that the white liberal cannot be trusted because he is identified with the white man's power structure and when the chips are down will support the white man's interests.

The consensus among Negro leaders is that the key to the problem of race relations is the refusal and inability of the white majority to understand the prevailing mood of the Negro minority. There is no escape from blackness for the Negro, they said, and this goes for all Negroes regardless of their station in life.

Thus a Negro girl with Caucasian features, a graduate cum laude from Vassar, recalled that whenever her white college friends held a party they included her but always invited a Negro man as her escort. She knows this was done out of kindness, but to the Negro girl it meant there was no escape for her from her race. Now she is Negro-conscious and is working actively on racial problems.

Although Malcolm X regards the Negro Christian Ministry as an evil influence, he found it politically expedient to share the same platform with Representative Adam Clayton Powell, who is pastor of the Abyssian Baptist Church, one of the largest Protestant congregations in the United States.

Malcolm X had no compunction on this score because Mr. Powell shares his opposition to whites in policy-making positions in Negro civil rights organizations.

Negro leaders believe there are other clues indicating a tactical shift by the Black Muslims to exploit the old-line Negro organizations.

Muhammed Speaks, the Black Muslim newspaper, has begun to report Mr. Powell's speeches with approval. It also published a lengthy interview with A. Philip Randolph, president of the Sleeping Car Porters Union.

There is no doubt in Mr. Farmer's mind that Malcolm X is beginning to emerge as a political power. Interviewed last Sunday on the WINS program, "News Conference," Mr. Farmer suggested that Mr. Powell might consider the Black Muslims a political threat to him and that this fear might explain his friendly public attitude toward Malcolm X.

Regardless of tactical shifts Malcolm X remains firm on one point:

"You cannot integrate the Negroes and the whites without bloodshed. It can't be done. The only peaceful way is for the Negroes and whites to separate."

Malcolm X Starting Drive in Washington

BY M. S. HANDLER | MAY 10, 1963

WASHINGTON, MAY 9 — Malcolm X arrived today to take over the leadership of the Black Muslim movement in the capital, where race relations have been causing anxiety.

Malcolm X said that he would continue as the leader of the movement in New York City and that he would maintain a home there as well as here. The local Black Muslim leader has been relieved of his duties because leaders of the movement say that he is unable to expand the movement in Washington.

Malcolm X described race relations in the nation as explosive. He said that unless the white majority acted swiftly to extend full civil rights to Negroes the situation could culminate in bloodshed. The extent of the Muslim movement here is a matter of speculation; the group declines to disclose its size. However, it maintains a mosque on Fourth Street, N.W.

"Birmingham," Malcolm X contended, "is an example of what can happen when the Negroes rely on the whites to solve their problems for them. The whites will never open the doors to the Negroes, who must learn to stand on their own feet, rely on themselves to improve their human condition. It is only by separating themselves from the white majority and leading their own lives that the Negroes can avoid situations which produce Birminghams."

The Black Muslim leader said that "the Negroes in this country are fed up with their lot and the refusal of the whites to give them their rights."

"When a situation has reached the point that it has in Birmingham something must give," he said. "It can't continue."

Malcolm X said that he intended to conduct all-Negro mass meetings each Sunday evening in Washington. By excluding whites, he asserted, the Negroes can discuss their problem without embarrassment, and reach the necessary conclusions. Fifty-four per cent of this city's 752,956 persons are Negroes, according to the Census of 1962.

The solution for the Negroes in Washington, according to Malcolm X, is to embrace Islam, the religion of the Moslems. Elijah Muhammed, the national leader, has suppressed alcohol, prostitution, narcotics, juvenile delinquency and crime among his followers, Malcolm X said. This behavior pattern, and not that offered by Christianity, is the one for the Negroes, he continued.

"By 1970, 90 per cent of the Negroes will be converted to Islam. Christianity is a white man's religion. It is always emphasing the role of the white man. Islam does not recognize color; it only recognizes the human personality," he said.

The leaders of the established Negro organizations, Malcolm asserted, have performed poorly, judged by results on civil rights.

"We [the Black Muslims] don't do a lot of talking. We shall be judged by our performance," he said, continuing:

We don't preach hatred and violence. But we believe that if a four-legged or two-legged dog attacks a Negro he should be killed. We only believe in defending ourselves against attack. What is hatred? We are only telling the truth about how the white man treats the black man.

Elijah Muhammed has a plan to separate the 20,000,000 Negroes from the white majority, but it is for him to speak. If the Negroes can't return to Africa and can't get their rights here, there should be a divorce with a property settlement. That means the Negroes should receive a part of this country where they can live their own lives.

Malcolm X Disputes Nonviolence Policy

BY THE NEW YORK TIMES | JUNE 5, 1963

MALCOLM X, THE Eastern leader of the Black Muslim movement, charged last night that the Rev. Dr. Martin Luther King Jr.'s policy of nonviolence was "disarming" Negroes in their struggle for rights.

"The followers of Martin Luther King will cut each other from head to foot, but they will not do anything to defend themselves against the attacks of the white man," Malcolm X said in a television interview.

The interview, with Dr. Kenneth Clark, a professor of psychology at City College of New York, was recorded on tape for broadcast last night over stations WNDT in New York City and WGBH in Boston.

"King is the best weapon that the white man, who wants to brutalize Negroes, has ever gotten in this country, because he is setting up a situation where, when the white man wants to attack Negroes, they can't defend themselves because King has put this foolish philosophy — you're not supposed to fight or you're not supposed to defend yourself."

He said followers of Elijah Muhammad, the leader of the Muslim movement, "don't advocate violence, but Mr. Muhammad does teach us that any human being who is intelligent has the right to defend himself."

Malcolm X Tells Rally in Harlem Kennedy Fails to Help Negroes

BY THOMAS P. RONAN | JUNE 30, 1963

MALCOLM X, A leader of the Black Muslim movement, assailed President Kennedy yesterday for talking about freedom in Europe "when 20,000,000 black men have no freedom here."

He told a Harlem street rally that Mr. Kennedy wanted to be President of Germany and of Ireland but that he had "no time to be President here."

"Right now representatives of the American Government are in Nazi Germany complaining about the Berlin wall, but they haven't done anything about the Alabama wall," he asserted.

The Black Muslims had given the rally advance billing as the largest of the year in Harlem, but the attendance was relatively small. At its height, when Malcolm X was speaking, a police official estimated the crowd at 2,000, but other observers thought that estimate was generous.

Hundreds of Negroes strolled and shopped on nearby streets as on any other Saturday afternoon while Malcolm X spoke from a platform on Lenox Avenue near the southeast corner of 115th Street.

The police had cut off northbound traffic between 112th and 116th Streets but southbound traffic moved freely. A detail of policemen was on duty at the scene, and others were held in reserve at nearby precincts.

On both sides of the avenue policemen and members of the movement appeared on roofs. When asked why the Black Muslims were there, a member of the organization said: "Just to see that everything is all right."

The meeting was scheduled to start at 3 P.M. but Malcolm X did not arrive until 3:35. The crowd shouted and applauded soon after he began speaking.

He said that those who had come expecting the Black Muslims to "apologize for the deeds of the white man," or to tell them to love the white man or turn the cheek "to the brutality of the white man" had come to the wrong place.

He asserted that this was a white country, which professed to be dedicated to freedom, justice and equality, but that there was no freedom, justice or equality for black men.

Before the rally, Malcolm X had said he would use it to start a moral cleanup of Harlem. On this subject, he said it was the white man who controlled the narcotics traffic, prostitution and the sale of whisky in Harlem.

At this point he brought to the platform five well-dressed Negroes who, he said, had spent many years in institutions as narcotic addicts.

He said that they had "a monkey on their backs, a white monkey, but the white man didn't cure them." They were cured of the habit, he continued, after they joined his movement.

By embracing the religion of Islam, the Black Muslim belief, he said, other Negroes could rehabilitate themselves, rise above the white man and run their affairs themselves in a separate state.

Malcolm X Silenced for Remarks on Assassination of Kennedy

BY R. W. APPLE JR. | DEC. 5, 1963

MALCOLM X, A leader of the Black Muslim movement, was suspended yesterday because of a speech in which he mocked the assassination of President Kennedy.

The action was taken by the group's ruler, Elijah Muhammad, who said Malcolm's remarks were an inaccurate reflection of Muslim attitudes. "With the rest of the world," he declared, "we are very shocked at the assassination of our President."

In a speech last Sunday at Manhattan Center, Malcolm said that Mr. Kennedy's death was a case of "the chickens coming home to roost." Amid laughter and applause from his followers in the audience, he added:

"Being an old farm boy myself, chickens coming home to roost never did make me sad; they've always made me glad."

Yesterday, he seemed contrite. "I shouldn't have said what I said," he conceded. "Anything that Mr. Muhammad does is all right with me; I believe absolutely in his wisdom and his authority."

Malcolm said he had learned of the suspension in Chicago on Monday in a conversation with Mr. Muhammad. "I will continue to administer the affairs of my mosque," he went on, "which is enough to occupy me."

He was critical of an article about his speech in The New York Times. "It took all the salt out of the bread and presented only the salt," he said. "But the salt should never have been there."

Malcolm, the New York and Washington leader of the movement, has been generally regarded as its second most powerful figure. It is he who is most often quoted in accounts of Muslim activities.

Many of his disciples have been saying recently, in fact, that Malcolm is exerting more influence than Mr. Muhammad himself.

There have also been reports of a rivalry between Malcolm and Mr. Muhammad's son-in-law, Raymond Sharrieff, who commands the secret army known as the Fruit of Islam. Both men, it is said, are eager to succeed the ruler.

Reached by telephone at his winter home in Phoenix, Ariz., Mr. Muhammad declined to discuss the possibility of dissension within the movement.

"Malcolm is still a minister," said the man who calls himself the Messenger of Allah, "but he will not be permitted to speak in public. I have rebuked him because he has not followed the way of Islam."

Asked when the suspension might be lifted, Mr. Muhammad replied, somewhat hesitantly: "I would not say. I will decide." He declined further comment on the action.

The Black Muslims are dedicated to the establishment of a Negro nation in America.

No one knows how many there are. The organization itself has never published membership figures, and the estimates of outsiders have varied from 25,000 to 250,000.

Almost all Muslim affairs are conducted in secret, but it is known that they have large real estate holdings in New York, Chicago, Detroit and Philadelphia.

Malcolm X has won a reputation for shrewdness and eloquence during his 15-year career in the movement. An ex-convict — he was a Harlem racketeer while still in his teens — he once said:

"I am not ashamed of this because it was all done when I was part of the white man's Christian world. As a Muslim, I would never have done these awful things that caused me to go to prison."

Malcolm X Flees Firebomb Attack

BY M. S. HANDLER | FEB. 15, 1965

MALCOLM X, THE controversial Black Nationalist leader, and his family escaped injury early yesterday when a firebomb attack wrecked the small brick house in which they lived in East Elmhurst, Queens.

Two, or possibly three, bottles of gasoline with fuses were hurled through the windows of the living room. They exploded and set fire to the house, at 23-11 97th Street.

Malcolm X had returned from a visit to France and England Saturday afternoon. He and his wife and four daughters were sleeping in bedrooms down a hall about 10 feet from the living room. The Molotov Cocktails crashed through the windows and exploded at about 2:45 A.M.

Malcolm X said he was awakened by the first explosion. He rushed his wife and children through the kitchen door into a small paved areaway behind the house and out of the range of the fire.

The blaze was quickly extinguished by the Fire Department, which, together with the Police Department bomb squad, opened an investigation. In the absence of firm clues, it was assumed that the firebombs were thrown from a passing automobile.

The house has been the subject of a prolonged controversy between Malcolm X and the Chicago-based Black Muslim movement, of which he is the former New York representative. The Black Muslims hold title to the house. They demanded Malcolm vacate it when he broke with them to found his own organization.

A civil court ruling gave Malcolm until Jan. 31 to vacate, but he appealed for a stay. A decision on the appeal is scheduled for today.

Malcolm's wife, Betty, and his daughters — Attilah, 6; Qubilah, 4; Ilyasah, 2, and 5-month-old Gamilah — were given shelter by neighbors yesterday. Later Malcolm and his wife returned to collect the few personal possessions that survived the fire. Then the Black Nationalist left for Detroit to keep a speaking engagement.

In a telephone interview, Malcolm said in Detroit that the attack could have come from several quarters — supporters of the Black Muslims or of the Ku Klux Klan, which he has been attacking in the South, or related groups. Malcolm recently visited Selma, where he attacked the Klan and other groups.

Malcolm said that he and his wife had been receiving anonymous telephoned threats daily for some time.

He said that he was awakened yesterday by an explosion and that, as best as he could remember, there were two or possibly three detonations.

The house is a modest one. It consists of a small living room, a dining room, two tiny bedrooms, a former utility room used for the baby's crib, a bathroom and kitchen. There is a small room under the gabled roof. There is also a small garage behind the areaway.

Malcolm was the center of incidents in France and Britain before returning to New York last Saturday. The French immigration police refused him permission to land at the Paris airfield and sent him back to England.

In Britain, he was taken on a tour of Smethwick, an area that has had racial problems, by the British Broadcasting Corporation. The B.B.C. was criticized by some for the tour.

Malcolm X Shot to Death at Rally Here

BY PETER KIHSS | FEB. 22, 1965

MALCOLM X, THE 39-year-old leader of a militant black nationalist movement, was shot to death yesterday afternoon at a rally of his followers in a ballroom in Washington Heights.

Shortly before midnight, a 22-year-old Negro, Thomas Hagan, was charged with the killing. The police rescued him from the ballroom crowd after he had been shot and beaten.

Malcolm, a bearded extremist, had said only a few words of greeting when a fusillade rang out. The bullets knocked him over backward.

Pandemonium broke out among the 400 Negroes in the Audubon Ballroom at 166th Street and Broadway. As men, women and children ducked under tables and flattened themselves on the floor, more shots were fired. Some witnesses said 30 shots had been fired.

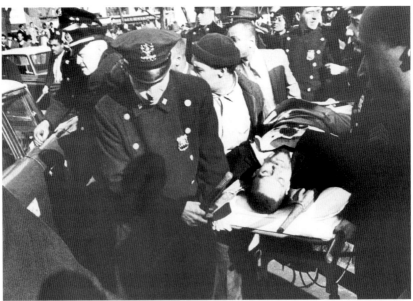

UNDERWOOD ARCHIVES/GETTY IMAGES

Malcolm X being taken to the hospital from the Audubon Ballroom yesterday after he was shot while addressing a meeting.

3 WEAPONS FIRED

The police said seven bullets had struck Malcolm. Three other Negroes were shot.

About two hours later the police said the shooting had apparently been a result of a feud between followers of Malcolm and members of the extremist group he broke with last year, the Black Muslims. However, the police declined to say whether Hagan is a Muslim.

The Medical Examiner's office said early this morning that a preliminary autopsy showed Malcolm had died of "multiple gunshot wounds." The office said that bullets of two different calibers as well as shotgun pellets had been removed from his body.

One police theory was that as many as five conspirators might have been involved, two creating a diversionary disturbance.

Hagan was shot in the left thigh and his left leg was broken apparently by kicks. He was under treatment in the Bellevue Hospital prison ward last night; perhaps a dozen policemen were guarding him, according to the hospital's night superintendent. The police said they had found a cartridge case with four unused .45-caliber shells in his pocket.

Two other Negroes, described as "apparent spectators" by Assistant Chief Inspector Harry Taylor, in command of Manhattan North uniformed police, also were shot. They were identified as William Harris, wounded seriously in the abdomen, and William Parker, shot in a foot. Both were taken to Columbia Presbyterian Medical Center, which is close to the ballroom.

Capt. Paul Glaser of the Police Department's Community Relations Bureau said early today that Hagan, using a double-barrelled shotgun with shortened barrels and stock, had killed Malcolm X.

Malcolm, a slim, reddish-haired six-footer with a gift for bitter eloquence against what he considered white exploitation of Negroes, broke in March, 1964, with the Black Muslim movement called the Nation of Islam, headed by Elijah Muhammad.

A weapon described as a 12-gauge shotgun was found behind the ballroom stage wrapped in a man's dark gray jacket.

As Hagan fired at Malcolm, Captain Glaser said, Reuben Francis, a follower of Malcolm, drew a .45-caliber automatic pistol and shot Hagan in the leg.

Francis, 33, of 871 East 179th Street, the Bronx, was charged with felonious assault and violation of the Sullivan Law.

Records of the Federal Bureau of Investigation showed that Hagan's real name is Talmadge Hayer, the police said this morning. He was booked as Thomas Hagan.

The F.B.I. records showed that the suspect's address was 347 Marshall Street, Paterson, N.J. He was arrested Nov. 7, 1963, the records showed, in Passaic for possession of stolen property.

Sanford Garelick, Assistant Chief Inspector in charge of the police Central Office Bureau and Squads, said at 5 P.M. — not quite two hours after the shooting — that "this is the result, it would seem, of a long-standing feud between the followers of Elijah Muhammad and the people who broke away from him, headed by Malcolm X."

At 7:30 P.M., Chief of Detectives Philip J. Walsh, who interrupted a vacation to join the hunt for the assassins, predicted "a long drawn-out investigation."

MUSLIM DENIES INVOLVEMENT

James X, New York spokesman for the Black Muslims, denied that his organization had had anything to do with the killing.

Just one week before the slaying, Malcolm was bombed out of the small brick home in East Elmhurst, Queens, where he had been living. James X suggested that Malcolm had set off firebombs himself "to get publicity."

Assemblyman Percy Sutton, Malcolm's lawyer, said the murdered leader had planned to disclose at yesterday's rally, "the names of those who were trying to kill him."

Mr. Sutton added that Malcolm had taken to carrying a pistol "because he feared for his life" and had notified the police by telephone that he was doing so even though he did not have a permit. Assistant

Chief Inspector Taylor, however, said Malcolm was unarmed when he was shot.

Chief Walsh said he believed "proper action was taken on all considerations of protection" for Malcolm, and "many of our requests in this connection were turned down."

Caption Glaser said that since Jan. 27 Malcolm had been offered police protection on seven different occasions, but had refused the guards each time.

REMARKS CRITICIZED

One factor in Malcolm's break with the Black Muslims was his comment on the assassination of President Kennedy. He called it a case of "chickens coming home to roost" and an outgrowth of violence that whites had used against Negroes. He was suspended by Elijah Muhammad and then started his own movement.

While the Nation of Islam searches for weapons anyone attending its meeting, Malcolm's new movement emphasized self-defense even with weapons. And so there was no search of anyone at yesterday's rally, a regular Sunday affair of Malcolm's Organization of Afro-American Unity. White persons were barred.

The Audubon Ballroom is in a two-story building on the south side of West 166th Street between Broadway and St. Nicholas Avenue, opposite a small park.

The meeting had been called for 2:30 P.M. in the second-floor hall, where 400 folding wooden chairs had been set up with two aisles going down the sides but no center aisle. At the back of the stage was a mural of a restful country scene.

'WOULD GIVE HIS LIFE'

Witnesses said one of the speakers who preceded Malcolm had asserted: "Malcolm is a man who would give his life for you."

Gene Simpson, a WMCA newsman, said he was sitting in the front row when Malcolm was introduced. He said Malcolm gave the traditional Arabic greeting, "Salaam Aleikum" — "peace be unto you."

"The crowd responded, 'Aleikum Salaam,' " Mr. Simpson said, "and then there was some disturbance about eight rows back. Everybody turned, and so did I, and then I heard Malcolm saying, 'Be cool now, don't get excited.'

"And then I heard this muffled sound, and I saw Malcolm hit with his hands still raised, and then he fell back over the chairs behind him. And everybody was shouting, and I saw one man firing a gun from under his coat behind me as I hit it [the floor] too.

"And then he was firing like he was in some Western, running backward toward the door and firing at the same time."

Sharon Six X Shabazz, 19, of 217 Bainbridge Street, who said she was a member of Malcolm's organization, told this story:

"I think he only said 'Brothers and Sisters' when there was a commotion in the back of the room. I thought it was some rowdy drunks."

Some one ran toward the stage, she said, there were loud noises, and she saw blood on Malcolm's face.

"Then everybody started screaming and running and he fell down," she said. "There was blood on his chest, too."

Stanley Scott, a United Press International reporter, said he had been admitted with this admonition by a Malcolm lieutenant: "As a Negro, you will be allowed to enter as a citizen if you like, but you must remove your press badge."

After Malcolm stepped to the rostrum and said a few words, Mr. Scott reported, "there was a scuffle at the back of the auditorium, possibly to distract attention from the assassins."

"Shots rang out," Mr. Scott went on. "Men, women and children ran for cover. They stretched out on the floor and ducked under tables.

"His wife, Betty, who was in the audience, ran about screaming hysterically, 'They're killing my husband!' "

A woman who was wearing a green scarf and a black felt hat with little floral buds, and who would identify herself only as a registered nurse, said she had seen "two men rushing toward the stage and firing from underneath their coats." One, she said, wore a tweed coat.

RUSHED TO THE STAGE

"I rushed to the stage even while the firing was going on," she said. "I don't know how I got on the stage, but I threw myself down on who I thought was Malcolm — but it wasn't. I was willing to die for the man. I would have taken the bullets myself. Then I saw Malcolm, and the firing had stopped, and I tried to give him artificial respiration.

"I think he was dead then."

Witnesses differed on the number of shots; some said as many as 30. Assistant Chief Inspector Taylor estimated the number at nearer eight. Six shots hit Malcolm in the chest and one hit him on the chin; some of the shots struck Malcolm after piercing the plywood rostrum in front of him.

Sgt. Alvin Aronoff and Patrolman Louis Angelos, who were in a radio car, heard the shooting. Sergeant Aronoff said he and his partner got to the ballroom just in time to see four or five persons run out, followed by a mob of perhaps 150, many of them pummeling Hagan.

"I've been shot — help me!" he quoted Hagan as shouting. The sergeant said he fired a warning shot into the air to halt the crowd, then pushed Hagan into the police car and drove him to the Wadsworth Avenue station house. From there the wounded man was quickly taken to Jewish Memorial Hospital and later to the Bellevue prison ward.

"In the car, I found four unused .45 cartridges in Hagan's pocket," Sergeant Aronoff said.

Malcolm was placed on a stretcher and wheeled one block up Broadway to the Vanderbilt Clinic emergency entrance at 167th Street. It was about 3:15 P.M., a Columbia Presbyterian Medical Center spokesman said later, when he reached a third-floor emergency operating room.

A team of doctors cut through his chest to massage his heart. But Malcolm was "either dead or in a death-appearing state," the spokesman said. The effort was given up at 3:30 P.M.

"The person you know as Malcolm X is dead," the spokesman reported.

Malcolm's birth name was Malcolm Little. He considered it a "slave name" and abandoned it when he joined the Black Muslims. At the hospital he was first listed as "John Doe" because he had not been officially identified.

The other wounded men, in addition to Hagan, were believed to have been hit by random shots. Parker was described as being 36 years old and living at 23-05 Thirtieth Avenue, Astoria, Queens. Harris's age was given as 51, and his address as 614 Oak Tree Place, Brooklyn.

The police declined to discuss any suspects.

Patrolman Thomas Hoy, 22, said he had been stationed outside the 166th Street entrance when "I heard the shooting, and the place exploded." He rushed in, saw Malcolm lying on the stage and "grabbed a suspect" who, he said, some people were chasing.

"As I brought him to the front of the ballroom, the crowd began beating me and the suspect," Patrolman Hoy said. He said he put this man — not otherwise identified later for newsmen — into a police car to be taken to the Wadsworth Avenue station.

At the station house later, one man said he had told investigators he believed the killers were "two short fellows, about 5 foot 6," who had been in the audience and who had walked toward the stage with their hands in their pockets.

This witness said he believed the men fired five or six shots from pistols when they were only about eight feet from Malcolm.

An alarm was issued for a 1963 blue Oldsmobile with a New York license plate 1G 2220. The police said the car was registered in the name of a Muslim Mosque, 23-11 97th Street, East Elmhurst, Queens, which was the address of the home Malcolm had occupied until it was burned. The Nation of Islam had him evicted by a Civil Court last week.

According to the police, Malcolm, his wife Betty and their four children moved last week into the Theresa Hotel, 125th Street and Seventh

Avenue, and then into the New York Hilton Hotel, Avenue of the Americas and 53d Street. They checked out at noon yesterday, the police said.

The couple was married in January, 1958, in Lansing, Mich. The children are Attilah, 6; Quiblah, 4, and Lamumbah, 5 months, all daughters, and Llyasah, a son, 2.

The widow held a brief press conference last night at George's Supper Club, 103-04 Astoria Boulevard, East Elmhurst. She said her husband had received telephone calls at the Hilton Saturday night and yesterday morning saying he had "better wake up before it's too late."

Malcolm's widow, who stayed at an undisclosed site in Elmhurst under police protection last night, was not questioned by the police on the killing.

Assemblyman Sutton, the family lawyer, said:

"Malcolm X died broke, without even an insurance policy. Every penny that he received from books, magazine articles and so on was assigned to the Black Muslims before he broke with them, and after that to the Muslim Mosque, Inc." — the sect Malcolm set up at the Theresa Hotel.

Extra policemen were on duty in Harlem and upper Manhattan yesterday and last night.

At 7:15 P.M. the police left the ballroom. Three cleaning women scrubbed blood off the stage, and overturned chairs were cleared away.

Musical instruments were placed on the stage and a dance sponsored by the Metro Associates, of 230 Tompkins Avenue, Brooklyn, went on as scheduled at 11 P.M.

Malcolm X Lived in 2 Worlds, White and Black, Both Bitter

BY PHILIP BENJAMIN | FEB. 22, 1965

HE WAS MALCOLM LITTLE, alias Big Red, a marijuana-smoking, cocaine-sniffing, zoot-suited, hip-talking hoodlum when he went to prison in 1946.

When he went free seven years later he was Malcolm X, an ascetic, a Black Muslim, a highly articulate man who hated the white world — a world he never made, but by whose standards he said he had lived.

Yesterday the Black Nationalist leader, who broke away last year from the Black Muslims of Elijah Muhammad, was shot dead as he prepared to speak at a rally in Harlem.

"Christianity took me to prison and Islam brought me out," Malcolm X used to say. He had no apologies for his criminal record, he said, "because it was all done when I was part of the white man's Christian world."

He was born in Omaha, on May 19, 1925, the son of the Rev. Earl Little, a 6-foot, 4-inch man who preached the back-to-Africa movement of Marcus Garvey, a Jamaican Negro who died in 1940.

His mother was a West Indian whose father was white. From this "white devil" grandfather Malcolm X got his reddish-brown complexion and reddish-brown hair.

TOLD OF HATE

"I hate every drop of that white rapist's blood that is in me," Malcolm once wrote.

The Little family, including 11 children, moved to Lansing, Mich. Malcolm's earliest vivid memory was seeing, at the age of 4, his house being burned to the ground by white racists. When he was 6 his father was killed under the wheels of a streetcar. Malcolm always believed his father had been murdered — first bludgeoned and then laid across the tracks.

The family broke up and Malcolm was sent to a state institution and was enrolled in the local public school at Mason, Mich. He was the only Negro student and his grades were among the highest in his class.

But after the eighth grade he left school and took a bus to Boston to live with a sister. In Boston and later in New York he drifted into the "cool" world; he drank, smoked marijuana and had an affair with a white woman. He became a waiter at Small's Paradise, a Harlem night club.

He was Big Red because he stood well over 6 feet and his hair was rust-colored. Big Red steered white men to Negro prostitutes and Negro men to white prostitutes; he sold marijuana, ran numbers, carried a pistol — in short, he was a hustler.

His cocaine habit cost him $20 a day and to support it he became a burglar. He was arrested in Boston after a series of burglaries there and was sent to the state prison at Charlestown. He was not quite 21 years old.

While he was in prison his sisters and brothers wrote to him about a "new" religion, Islam, preached to black men in the United States by the Honorable Elijah Muhammad, formerly Elijah Poole. The core of his teaching was the superiority of the black man, who was the first man on earth; the whites came later, a "devil" race.

Malcolm began to correspond with Elijah Muhammad, and when he left prison he was a Black Muslim. He no longer bore the surname of Little, because, as with nearly all American Negro surnames, it belonged to the white slave owners.

He went to Chicago, where Elijah Muhammad had his headquarters and as eagerly as he had entered the "cool" world he entered the ascetic world. He gave up pork, tobacco, alcohol, marijuana, cocaine, gambling, dancing, movies, sports and promiscuity.

Elijah Muhammad recognized almost at once that he had in Malcolm a man of intelligence and authority. He sent him on speaking tours around the country, and eventually Malcolm came to New York to take over Mosque No. 7, then a small, voiceless and ineffectual group.

In ordinary conversation he was quiet, pleasant, articulate and even humorous. His accent was Midwestern. On the public platform his quality was cold fury; his eyes burned behind horn-rimmed glasses. In a few years he built up Mosque Seven. In 1958 he married a member of the mosque, Sister Betty X, and they had four children.

HE WAS ONCE A RACIST

By his own admission, he had once been a racist, an advocate of black separatism. But after he broke with Elijah Muhammad last year, he said he had turned away from racism. That break came after the assassination of President Kennedy. Malcolm X had said the assassination was a case of "chickens coming home to roost."

For this remark Elijah Muhammad suspended Malcolm X, and the break was never healed. Malcolm set up the Muslim Mosque, Inc., with headquarters at the Theresa Hotel at 125th Street and Seventh Avenue. Last year he went to Mecca as a pilgrim. There, he said, he had been impressed by the "brotherhood, the people of all races, all colors coming together as one."

Two weeks ago he visited Britain — on a passport issued to Malcolm Little — and went to Smethwick, a town near Birmingham with a large colored population. His tour of Smethwick was criticized by some residents as an attempt to fan racism.

His home in Queens was bombed a week ago, and he accused the Black Muslims of doing it.

Writing in the Saturday Evening Post last year he said: "Some of the followers of Elijah Muhammad would still consider it a first-rank honor to kill me. Also I know that any day, any night, I could die at the hands of some white devil racists. … I dream that one day history will look upon me as having been one of the voices that perhaps helped to save America from a grave, even possibly fatal catastrophe."

The Voice of Malcolm X Has an Audience Again

BY C. GERALD FRASER | FEB. 20, 1990

TWENTY-FIVE YEARS AFTER Malcolm X was assassinated, his voice is being heard again, his ideology is being re-examined and his face adorns T-shirts and buttons.

One reason is that "a young generation is finding in Malcolm an excruciating critique of the racism, drugs and violence in society," said Ron Daniels, a consultant in community development and a member of the newly formed National Malcolm X Commemoration Commission.

The young generation, he added, "also finds comfort in Malcolm's willingness to challenge the system, to affirm his identity and identify with Africa."

To further an understanding of Malcolm, the black nationalist who as a spokesman for the Nation of Islam, or Black Muslims, preached defiance and self-defense in the face of racism, the commission has organized programs across the country tomorrow, the 25th anniversary of Malcolm X's murder in the Audubon Ballroom in the Washington Heights section of Manhattan.

MALCOLM THE TENTH?

The programs will underscore a significant shift from only a few years ago when Malcolm's name was rarely recognized by the young — when a popular anecdote being repeated told of a black college student asking, "Who was Malcolm the Tenth?"

But the commission members say that today, with Malcolm's voice being heard on such popular rap songs as "Self Destruction" by the group Stop the Violence Movement, most people are asking not who Malcolm was, but what did he say.

Cheryll Y. Greene, the executive editor of Essence, the magazine for black women, said people are finding that "Malcolm has many answers that are as relevant today as they were in the 1960's." She also said that the renewed interest in Malcolm X is partly due to men "trying to reassert themselves in the struggle and looking to Malcolm because he was a consummate figure of male strength."

In the last three years, copies of Malcolm X's speeches have been in increasing demand, said Steve Clarke of Pathfinder Press, the major distributor of English-language editions of collections of Malcolm's speeches. In the last 20 years, Pathfinder has sold more than 500,000 books by and about Malcolm X, and since July it has sold 33,000 copies of its most recent of seven titles, "Malcolm X: The Last Speeches."

Mr. Clarke said that in recent years Malcolm's "standing as a hero, as a great revolutionary figure," has grown and that "efforts to picture him as a hatemonger have been transformed, not only by blacks but more broadly."

"White and Latino youth are also interested in him," Mr. Clarke said.

SERVICES ON WEDNESDAY

Last year, observing Malcolm's 64th-birthday anniversary, scholars met at the Schomburg Center for Research in Black Culture in Harlem to discuss his life and speeches. Joined by many literary figures, some of the scholars formed the national commission to focus the attention of blacks on "the life, the legacy, the lessons" of Malcolm X, whose formal Muslim name was El Hajj Malik el-Shabazz.

Born as Malcolm Little on May 19, 1925, in Omaha, Neb., he converted to Islam in prison in the late 1940's and became the Nation of Islam's spokesman. But disputes with the Nation's leader, Elijah Muhammad, in 1963 led Malcolm to found his own group, the Organization of Afro-American Unity. He was said to have been killed by three members of the Nation of Islam.

The commission has also organized a memorial service at the Abyssinian Baptist Church in Harlem and a discussion at the Shiloh Baptist Church's Family Life Center in Washington.

The Harlem program, from 6:30 to 9:30 P.M. tomorrow, will include Malcolm X's widow, Dr. Betty Shabazz; the poet and playwright Amiri Baraka; the film maker Spike Lee; Percy E. Sutton, the former Manhattan Borough President who was Malcolm X's lawyer, and Chuck D. of the rap group Public Enemy.

The Washington program will feature Professor Ron Walters of Howard University and the Rev. Jesse Jackson.

A 'DAY OF COMMEMORATION'

A. Peter Bailey, a writer and commission member who describes himself as "still a Malcolmite after all these years," was a member of Malcolm's Organization of Afro-American Unity and was present when Malcolm was killed. He said he hoped that two aspects of Malcolm X's legacy could be set right.

"One is philosophical — Malcolm X versus Martin Luther King," he said. A misconception, he said, is that unlike Dr. King, Malcolm advocated violence as a means to fight racism and discrimination. "It was not nonviolence versus violence, but nonviolence versus self-defense," Mr. Bailey said. To pit Dr. King's philosophy of nonviolence against Malcolm's purported creed of violence was "a distortion of Malcolm's position," Mr. Bailey said.

"He, Malcolm, consistently talked self-defense," Mr. Bailey said. "The media distorted the argument."

The second clarification Mr. Bailey wants is to put "Malcolm X's righteous anger into the context of the times, 1955 to 1965." Mr. Bailey said the civil-rights memorial in Montgomery, Ala., lists 40 people murdered from 1955 to 1965, including Medgar Evers and the four girls killed when a Birmingham church was bombed.

"Malcolm had a right to be angry — people being lynched and nobody being punished," Mr. Bailey said. "The press softened the violence against blacks. Malcolm expressed the righteous anger that most of us felt, but we were afraid to say it."

Young Believe Malcolm X Is Still Speaking to Them

BY ISABEL WILKERSON | NOV. 18, 1992

BOSTON, NOV. 12 — In a Roxbury high school near the streets where Malcolm X hustled away his adolescence, the 11 teen-agers in Steve Grace's history class sat straight and spellbound as the stark image of the Black Muslim leader glowed from a television set up front.

The gaunt man in the thin tie and spectacles was talking to 1960's Harlem about how drugs were destroying the community, how they were flown in by outsiders and how blacks needed to unite against the scourge — words that could as easily have been said of 1990's Roxbury.

The teen-agers nodded their heads in both agreement and awe, then pummeled their teacher with questions and testimonials.

A FOLK HERO

"You look at him, and you see how good of a man he was," Orlando Lang, a senior in the class, said with sadness. "He was taken away as if it was never meant for us to achieve."

For Spike Lee, whose movie opens Wednesday, Malcolm X may be a career-defining project. For T-shirt makers, Malcolm X may be a bonanza and recessionary godsend. But to black urban teen-agers whose daily routines include dodging bullets and fending off crack dealers and gang members, Malcolm X is their folk hero, the resurrected spokesman for an angry, jaded generation.

Malcolm X, assassinated in New York City 27 years ago, claims such status today because he was a blunt-talking black Everyman, a fast-forwarded, all-in-one version of black life in America, from poverty to street life to redemption.

In interviews with more than 50 inner-city teen-agers and young adults across the country, most spoke with dutiful respect for the Rev. Dr. Martin Luther King Jr., were neutral on the Rev. Jesse Jackson, could happily tick off the names of their favorite actors and athletes — but reserved their most passionate words for Malcolm X.

"He stood up to the white man and he had dignity doing it," said James Fuller, a junior at Fresno State University in California. "He was well educated, that's why whites hated him so much. He was educated and didn't take no mess. If I was in those days, I would have to go with Malcolm."

BOOST FOR READING

To be sure, the familiarity with Malcolm X varies widely, with some young people seizing only on his famous phrase, "By Any Means Necessary," and others caught up in the rebel-chic "X" wear and still others trying to steep themselves in his life story.

Still others, however, seem unable to read enough about the man. Malcolm X has apparently done what literacy programs, bookmobiles, librarians, English teachers and Barbara Bush have tried to do for years — get urban young people to read.

"I don't like to read, but when I first picked up this book I couldn't get my nose out of it," Verkeya Holman, an eighth grader at Frederick Douglass Academy in Harlem, said of "The Autobiography of Malcolm X."

The teen-age appetite for anything about the man has helped push the autobiography, published in 1964, onto the New York Times bestseller list for paperback nonfiction and sent parents scrambling to find obscure titles that their children demanded.

Urban libraries cannot keep the autobiography or "The Last Speeches" on the shelves. Malcolm X has become the No. 1 research subject in some predominantly black schools.

"It's like being introduced to ice cream for the first time," Mr. Grace, a social studies teacher at Madison Park High School in Roxbury, said of his students' fascination with Malcolm X. "The first thing they want to know is, 'Why wasn't I told about him, and how could you let him be killed?' "

Unlike the 1960's, Malcolm X's appeal has crossed racial barriers this time. But that has created another tug-of-war with some blacks feeling Malcolm X belongs to them and resenting whites wearing the paraphernalia. Some white teen-agers are drawn to the symbol but are afraid of its implications or want to see the movie but are afraid to be the only white in the theater.

Michael Gwinn, a senior at Evanston High School outside Chicago, who is white, said he would like to wear some "X" clothes, but added: "He's the black population's hero, and a white kid trying to take a part of that hero may not go over too well."

HELP FROM MOVIE

Of the many faces of Malcolm X, white students tend to focus on his racial harmony phase toward the end of his life, dismissing his anti-white diatribes as rhetorical devices to unite blacks, while black students appear drawn to those very diatribes, his calls for black self-reliance and his personal transformation.

The latter-day Malcolm-worship has been stoked by the extraordinary hype over Mr. Lee's movie, but it showed its first signs in 1990 when blacks began reassessing Malcolm X on the 25th anniversary of his death.

Rap groups wrote odes to him; teen-agers, black and white, began wearing anything with an "X" on it, and his words and image reappeared with a ubiquitousness that led Rasheed Ziyad, a Black Muslim who owns a convenience store in Watts, to say the other day, "It seems like Malcolm is more alive today than when he was alive."

There is perhaps no more fertile soil for his words than South-Central Los Angeles, still raw from the riots in April.

Entire blocks have been plowed flat, whole shopping centers leveled, jobs are still scarce, and black and Hispanic teen-agers say they are as isolated as ever.

Right after the riots, a mural went up at Locke High School in Watts. Students painted it to vent their feelings. It depicted a five-foot high portrait of Malcolm, a tear on his cheek, and a gigantic "X."

People figured it would be splattered with graffiti, like everything else, before the paint was dry.

"The mural has been up six months," said Barbara Blackman, the school librarian whose office window sits next to the mural. "The kids have not touched it. That's how much they respect him."

Said William Warner, a senior at the school: "We finally see something worth respecting. So we don't want to deface it."

They respect him as a no-nonsense man who spoke his mind and did not care whose toes he stepped on, whether it was racist whites or bourgeois blacks. And while he did not explicitly call for violence, he did not rule out self-defense at a time when blacks were routinely being sprayed with hoses and beaten by white sheriffs' deputies at peaceful demonstrations.

To many young people, Dr. King seems saintly and superhuman. Malcolm X is the big brother who took a wrong turn but got his life together. While Dr. King fashioned his oratory to appeal to whites, Malcolm X made no pretense that it was blacks he was trying to wake up. And if many blacks did not listen when he was alive, young blacks are listening now.

"The King theory is not what's happening in the 20th Century," Mr. Warner said. "We just don't hold hands and march anymore. We held hands and slapped tambourines and nothing happened."

The 17-year-old has finished the autobiography and is on to "The Last Speeches," and says that between the riots and his discovery of Malcolm X he has learned what really is at stake.

"Malcolm is saying that it's about power," Mr. Warner said. "We can go to school and study and try to get power. Or we can take it and get violent if you push us to the edge. If we get jobs and money, we'll march your march and talk your talk. It's not a black-white thing, it's a green thing."

RECITING THE LIFE

They like Malcolm X because he wasn't perfect and made something of his life anyway. His run-ins with the law, his zoot-suited, drug-peddling, juke-joint days only give him more credibility with young people.

Anthony Jackson, a senior at Locke High School, can recite the details of Malcolm X's life as if he is talking about himself. Sitting in the school library talking about Malcolm X, he could name the relatives, describe the poor childhood in Lansing and the wild days in Boston, the time spent reading the dictionary in jail and the conversion to life as an ascetic Muslim, father and black advocate.

"He gives you a sense of pride," said Anthony Jackson, a senior at Locke High School. "You don't have to have the bad experiences he had because he went through it for you."

Joe Thompson, another senior at Locke, said, "Malcolm X is my hero because he wasn't a punk."

Mr. Thompson said he had been stopped by gang members on his way home from school and has to worry about whose territory he is in. He said that Malcolm X would understand what he meant. "When you're raised up from a toddler around here," he said, "you have to do what you have to do to survive out there on the street."

HOSTILITY CONTINUES

The youthful embrace of Malcolm X is in stark contrast to the nagging ambivalence, hostility even, of the older generation.

In the lunch room of the Roxbury branch of New England Bell, a young man bearing Malcolm X's Arabic name, Malik, talked about how much he loved what his name stood for and how he thought Malcolm X was "a strong man who stood up for black people."

Just then, a black woman in her 50's, weighed in on the topic. "Martin Luther King was our god," said the woman, who declined to give her name. "Malcolm X was our devil."

In Lansing, Malcolm X's childhood home, 32 classes at Eastern High school are reading the autobiography and Malcolm X posters fill the halls and classrooms. But many older people, black and white, are trying to forget Malcolm X ever lived there.

They still see Malcolm X as being on the militant fringe. "He was so radical it was hard to hear him back then," said Robert T. Carter, an associate professor of psychology and education at Columbia University Teachers College in Manhattan. "In the end, Malcolm embraced the idea of coming together, but not in a 'Please would you let me' manner. Now we realize that Malcolm was right. We didn't listen then."

Now young people have taken up his appeal for equality "by any means necessary" as their generational motto.

A banner hanging in the front hall of the Roxbury Boys and Girls Club bears a huge "X" and the words "Education by Any Means Necessary."

Many school districts are ignoring the phenomenon. "Malcolm X had behavior that we don't like," said Dr. Bobbi Hentrel, associate principal of Brace Ledderly Elementary School in Southfield, Mich., outside Detroit. "He was violent. It is the opposite of what Martin Luther King stood for."

But other schools are immersing students in Malcolm X. Frederick Douglass Academy, a middle school in Harlem, is taking all 300 of its students to see the movie on Nov. 24.

The renewed acceptance of Malcolm X fits in with efforts of many blacks to embrace their heritage.

"Some of us are beginning to wake up," said Kishawn Anderson, a senior at Locke. "We're in a bottomless pit. We're becoming more conscious of what our people struggled through."

Malcolm X Letters Show His Evolution

BY THE NEW YORK TIMES | MARCH 8, 2002

IN A RARE TROVE of journals, letters and other writings attributed to Malcolm X that are to be auctioned on March 20, the fervid civil rights leader shows himself as humbled by his first pilgrimage to Mecca, in 1964, the year he broke with the Nation of Islam amid his growing conviction that not all whites were devils.

An entry dated April 17, 1964, describes the crowds praying at Mecca as being of "all colors, bowing in unison," and that, watching them, he was "not conscious of color (race) for the first time in my life." He added, "The whites don't seem white."

While many of these views were previously known from his autobiography, the documents offer fresh insights into the evolution of Malcolm X's thinking.

The documents, unearthed only recently after years in a storage unit in Florida, were previously unknown to scholars and historians. They were shown to reporters for the first time today at Butterfields auction house here before a three-day public viewing, followed next weekend by another showing in San Francisco, where the auction will take place.

Questioned as to the material's authenticity, Catherine Williamson, director of the fine books and manuscripts department at Butterfields, said simply, "We've done our homework."

Malcolm X's descendants are unhappy about the impending sale, and the auction house expects them to try to stop it. But at least two of the relatives have said that the material is real.

"Our position is that the documents are authentic," said Joseph Fleming, a lawyer who represents several of Malcolm X's six daughters. Rodnell P. Collins, a nephew of Malcolm X, said he recognized the material.

To enable a single buyer or institution to buy the collection outright, the auction house has decided to first offer it as a single lot. If the auctioneer's lowest price is not met, Butterfields will seek bids on each of the individual 21 lots, which are expected to bring in between $300,000 and $500,000.

The auction house will not identify the owner of the writings and other personal possessions other than to say he is a Florida resident who bought the material at a storage facility auction without initially knowing what it was.

In the first journal from Mecca, Malcolm X seemed to describe his growing belief that the militant path he had taken was not necessarily the correct one. "Out of the thick darkness comes sudden light," he wrote. "My, how fortune can change."

The next day, April 18, 1964, after a night he described as lonely, his spirits were revived by the prospect of the final stage of the pilgrimage:

"My excitement is indescribable. My window faces the sea, westward. The streets are filled with the incoming pilgrims from all over the world, the prayers of Allah and verses from the Quran are on the lips of everyone — never have I seen such a beautiful sight, nor witnessed such a scene, nor felt such an atmosphere."

After returning from his two trips to Africa and the Middle East that year, Malcolm X, whose original surname was Little, changed his name once again, to El-Hajj Malik El-Shabazz, and formed the Organization of Afro-American Unity, an act that took him out of the hard-line Nation of Islam orbit and which, many believe, led to his assassination in New York on Feb. 21, 1965.

Fifteen years earlier, writing to his brother Philbert from prison in Massachusetts, to which he had been sentenced on a robbery charge, Malcolm X wrote of his attempts to convert fellow inmates to Islam, and of being transferred to another facility as a result. "With expertly concocted and perpetuated lies, they made the youths even fear to be seen with me," he wrote. "The ones who did not fear the devil nor his tools were the ones who have grasped Islam the most firmly."

Yet four years earlier, in 1946, Malcolm X castigated his two brothers, who had converted to Islam, for trying to bring him into the fold.

"Under no circumstances don't ever preach to me," he wrote to Philbert from prison that year. "That sounds phony. All people who talk like that sound phony to me because I know that is all it is: just talk."

The documents and possessions include Malcolm X's copy of the Koran, a large number of speeches, photographs, handwritten drafts of radio addresses, airline tickets, receipts and business cards from his travels, and a 1959 letter to his wife, Betty, in which he sends her $20 that he hopes she will use "sparingly."

Malcolm X had said he had planned to write a book based on his journals.

Glossary

assassination The act of murdering someone for political reasons.

black nationalism A political and social movement in the United States promoting the interests and goals of African Americans who scorned integration and wanted an exclusively black republic.

civil disobedience The refusal of a citizen to obey certain laws, demands, orders or commands of the government.

civil rights Rights that ensure one's ability to participate in the civil and political life of a country without discrimination or oppression.

communist A person who supports the principles of communism, the political model wherein all property is publicly owned and each person is paid according to their abilities and needs.

demonstrator A participant in a public protest or march.

desegregation The policy of ending separation by race.

disorders States of unrest; sometimes indicates rioting, looting or vandalism.

enjoin To stop someone from performing an action.

injunction A legal court order stopping someone from pursuing an action.

integration An act or instance of combining separate groups into one group.

loot To steal goods from businesses or homes during a protest or riot.

militant An extreme, forceful approach in support of a cause.

racial discrimination The unfair treatment of different groups of people based on race.

resistance The refusal to accept or comply with something.

segregation Separation of racial groups in daily life.

Media Literacy Terms

"Media literacy" refers to the ability to access, understand, critically assess and create media. The following terms are important components of media literacy, and they will help you critically engage with the articles in this title.

angle The aspect of a news story on which a journalist focuses and develops.

attribution The method by which a source is identified or by which facts and information are assigned to the person who provided them.

balance Principle of journalism that both perspectives of an argument should be presented in a fair way.

chronological order Method of writing a story presenting the details of the story in the order in which they occurred.

commentary Type of story that is an expression of opinion on recent events by a journalist generally known as a commentator.

credibility The quality of being trustworthy and believable, said of a journalistic source.

critical review Type of story that describes an event or work of art, such as a theater performance, film, concert, book, restaurant, radio or television program, exhibition or musical piece, and offers critical assessment of its quality and reception.

editorial Article of opinion or interpretation.

feature story Article designed to entertain as well as to inform.

headline Type, usually 18 point or larger, used to introduce a story.

human interest story Type of story that focuses on individuals and how events or issues affect their lives, generally offering a sense of relatability to the reader.

impartiality Principle of journalism that a story should not reflect a journalist's bias and should contain balance.

intention The motive or reason behind something, such as the publication of a news story.

interview story Type of story in which the facts are gathered primarily by interviewing another person or persons.

motive The reason behind something, such as the publication of a news story or a source's perspective on an issue.

news story An article or style of expository writing that reports news, generally in a straightforward fashion and without editorial comment.

op-ed An opinion piece that reflects a prominent individual's opinion on a topic of interest.

paraphrase The summary of an individual's words, with attribution, rather than a direct quotation of their exact words.

quotation The use of an individual's exact words indicated by the use of quotation marks and proper attribution.

reliability The quality of being dependable and accurate, said of a journalistic source.

rhetorical device Technique in writing intending to persuade the reader or communicate a message from a certain perspective.

source The origin of the information reported in journalism.

style A distinctive use of language in writing or speech; also a news or publishing organization's rules for consistent use of language with regards to spelling, punctuation, typography and capitalization, usually regimented by a house style guide.

tone A manner of expression in writing or speech.

Media Literacy Questions

1. Identify the various sources cited in the article "27 Bi-Racial Bus Riders Jailed in Jackson, Miss., as They Widen Campaign" (on page 86). How does Claude Sitton attribute information to each of these sources in his article? How effective are Sitton's attributions in helping the reader identify his sources?

2. Compare the headlines of "Student From Little Rock" (on page 68) and "Malcolm X Lived in 2 Worlds, White and Black, Both Bitter" (on page 196). Which is a more compelling headline, and why? How could the less compelling headline be changed to better draw the reader's interest?

3. What type of story is "Spokesman for Negroes" (on page 121)? Can you identify another article in this collection that is the same type of story? What elements helped you come to your conclusion?

4. "200,000 March for Civil Rights in Orderly Washington Rally; President Sees Gain for Negro" (on page 127) features a photograph. What does this photograph add to the article?

5. Identify each of the sources in "Malcolm X Shot to Death at Rally Here" (on page 188) as a primary source or a secondary source. Evaluate the reliability and credibility of each source. How does your evaluation of each source change your perspective on this article?

6. Does Benjamin Fine demonstrate the journalistic principle of impartiality in his article "Little Rock Faces Showdown Today Over

Integration" (on page 20)? If so, how did he do so? If not, what could Fine have included to make his article more impartial?

7. Does "Montgomery Tension High After Threats of Bombing" (on page 77) use multiple sources? What are the strengths of using multiple sources in a journalistic piece? What are the weaknesses of relying heavily on only one or a few sources?

8. What is the intention of the article "Rights Leader's Undaunted Widow" (on page 151)? How effectively does it achieve its intended purpose?

9. Analyze the authors' reporting in "Negroes Say Conditions in U.S. Explain Nationalists' Militancy" (on page 164) and "Cultists on Coast Denounce Police" (on page 167). Do you think one journalist is more balanced in his reporting than the other? If so, why do you think so?

10. What type of story is "Malcolm X Silenced for Remarks on Assassination of Kennedy" (on page 184)? Can you identify another article in this collection that is the same type of story? What elements helped you come to your conclusion?

11. In "TV: Mrs. King Takes March Spotlight" (on page 156), Jack Gould paraphrases information from Coretta Scott King. What are the strengths of the use of a paraphrase as opposed to a direct quote? What are the weaknesses?

12. What is the intention of the article "How M.L.K.'s Death Helped Lead to Gun Control in the U.S." (on page 159)? How effectively does it achieve its intended purpose?

Citations

All citations in this list are formatted according to the
Modern Language Association's (MLA) style guide.

BOOK CITATION

THE NEW YORK TIMES EDITORIAL STAFF. *Civil Rights Advocates.* New York:
New York Times Educational Publishing, 2020.

ONLINE ARTICLE CITATIONS

APPLE, R. W., JR. "Malcolm X Silenced for Remarks on Assassination of
Kennedy." *The New York Times*, 5 Dec. 1963, www.timesmachine.nytimes
.com/timesmachine/1963/12/05/89983908.html.

BECKER, BILL. "Cultists on Coast Denounce Police." *The New York Times*,
6 May 1962, www.timesmachine.nytimes.com/timesmachine/1962/05
/06/94868983.html.

BENJAMIN, PHILIP. "Malcolm X Lived in 2 Worlds, White and Black, Both
Bitter." *The New York Times*, 22 Feb. 1965, www.timesmachine.nytimes
.com/timesmachine/1965/02/22/101528416.html.

FINE, BENJAMIN. "Arkansas Troops Bar Negro Pupils." *The New York Times*,
5 Sept. 1957, www.timesmachine.nytimes.com/timesmachine/1957/09
/05/121029344.html.

FINE, BENJAMIN. "Little Rock Faces Showdown Today Over Integration."
The New York Times, 7 Sept. 1957, www.timesmachine.nytimes.com
/timesmachine/1957/09/07/93216562.html.

FINE, BENJAMIN. "Militia Sent to Little Rock." *The New York Times*,
3 Sept. 1957, www.timesmachine.nytimes.com/timesmachine/1957
/09/03/91163355.html.

FINE, BENJAMIN. "9 in Little Rock Leave Unguarded." *The New York Times*,
24 Oct. 1957, www.timesmachine.nytimes.com/timesmachine/1957/10
/24/84778514.html.

FINE, BENJAMIN. "Students Accept Negroes Calmly." *The New York Times*, 26 Sept. 1957, www.timesmachine.nytimes.com/timesmachine/1957/09/26/93217095.html.

FINE, BENJAMIN. "Students Unhurt." *The New York Times*, 24 Sept. 1957, www.timesmachine.nytimes.com/timesmachine/1957/09/24/84765249.html.

FRASER, C. GERALD. "The Voice of Malcolm X Has an Audience Again." *The New York Times*, 20 Feb. 1990, www.nytimes.com/1990/02/20/nyregion/the-voice-of-malcolm-x-has-an-audience-again.html.

GOULD, JACK. "TV: Mrs. King Takes March Spotlight." *The New York Times*, 20 June 1968, https://timesmachine.nytimes.com/timesmachine/1968/06/20/77307954.html.

HALBERSTAM, DAVID. "Negro Girl a Force in Campaign; Encouraged Bus to Keep Rolling." *The New York Times*, 23 May 1961, www.timesmachine.nytimes.com/timesmachine/1961/05/23/97239561.html.

HANDLER, M. S. "Assertive Spirit Stirs Negroes, Puts Vigor in Civil Rights Drive." *The New York Times*, 23 Apr. 1963, www.timesmachine.nytimes.com/timesmachine/1963/04/23/81800577.html.

HANDLER, M. S. "Malcolm X Flees Firebomb Attack." *The New York Times*, 15 Feb. 1965, www.timesmachine.nytimes.com/timesmachine/1965/02/15/101527042.html.

HANDLER, M. S. "Malcolm X Starting Drive in Washington." *The New York Times*, 10 May 1963, www.timesmachine.nytimes.com/timesmachine/1963/05/10/82066656.html.

HUNT, RICHARD P. "2 'Freedom' Buses Linked by Youth." *The New York Times*, 22 May 1961, www.timesmachine.nytimes.com/timesmachine/1961/05/22/101464353.html.

KATZ, RALPH. "Dr. King Opening Negro Vote Drive." *The New York Times*, 26 Sept. 1961, www.timesmachine.nytimes.com/timesmachine/1961/09/26/118519307.html.

KENWORTHY, E. W. "Supreme Court Reaffirms Ban on Travel Segregation." *The New York Times*, 27 Feb. 1962, www.timesmachine.nytimes.com/timesmachine/1962/02/27/81785088.html.

KENWORTHY, E. W. "200,000 March for Civil Rights in Orderly Washington Rally; President Sees Gain for Negro." *The New York Times*, 29 Aug. 1963, www.timesmachine.nytimes.com/timesmachine/1963/08/29/89957615.html.

KIHSS, PETER. "Malcolm X Shot to Death at Rally Here". *The New York Times*,

22 Feb. 1965, www.timesmachine.nytimes.com/timesmachine
/1965/02/22/101528359.html.

LISSNER, WILL. "Bus Depots Vary in Racial Policy." *The New York Times*,
12 Nov. 1961, www.timesmachine.nytimes.com/timesmachine/1961/11
/12/101484682.html.

LOFTUS, JOSEPH A. "I.C.C. Orders End of Racial Curbs on Bus Travelers."
The New York Times, 23 Sept. 1961, www.timesmachine.nytimes.com
/timesmachine/1961/09/23/118927744.html.

THE NEW YORK TIMES. "Dr. King Is Freed." *The New York Times*, 19 Dec. 1961,
www.timesmachine.nytimes.com/timesmachine/1961/12/19/119433032.html.

THE NEW YORK TIMES. "Fighter for Integration: Daisy Getson Bates."
The New York Times, 24 Sept. 1957, www.timesmachine.nytimes
.com/timesmachine/1957/09/24/84765966.html.

THE NEW YORK TIMES. "Little Rock Faces New School Fight." *The New York
Times*, 31 May 1958, www.timesmachine.nytimes.com/timesmachine
/1958/05/31/81885008.html.

THE NEW YORK TIMES. "Little Rock Girl Sees More Strife." *The New York
Times*, 23 Feb. 1958, www.timesmachine.nytimes.com/timesmachine
/1958/02/23/89052515.html.

THE NEW YORK TIMES. "Malcolm X Disputes Nonviolence Policy." *The
New York Times*, 5 June 1963, www.timesmachine.nytimes.com
/timesmachine/1963/06/05/89533280.html.

THE NEW YORK TIMES. "Malcolm X Letters Show His Evolution." *The New York
Times*, 8 Mar. 2002, www.nytimes.com/2002/03/08/us/malcolm
-x-letters-show-his-evolution.html.

THE NEW YORK TIMES. "Mrs. King to Speak at Anti-Vietnam War Rally."
The New York Times, 19 Apr. 1968, www.timesmachine.nytimes.com
/timesmachine/1968/04/19/77083906.html.

THE NEW YORK TIMES. "President Urged to End Race Laws." *The New
York Times*, 6 June 1961, www.timesmachine.nytimes.com
/timesmachine/1961/06/06/118041173.html.

THE NEW YORK TIMES. "Rights Leader's Undaunted Widow." *The New York
Times*, 9 Apr. 1968, www.timesmachine.nytimes.com/timesmachine
/1968/04/09/88938579.html.

THE NEW YORK TIMES. "Spokesman for Negroes." *The New York Times*,
16 July 1962, www.timesmachine.nytimes.com/timesmachine
/1962/07/16/89879918.html.

OPPEL, RICHARD A., JR. "How M.L.K.'s Death Helped Lead to Gun Control in the U.S." *The New York Times*, 3 Apr. 2018, www.nytimes.com/2018/04/03 /us/martin-luther-king-1968-gun-control-act.html.

PARKE, RICHARD H. "189 Riders Appeal Jackson Conviction." *The New York Times*, 15 Aug. 1961, www.timesmachine.nytimes.com/timesmachine /1961/08/15/97614713.html.

PORTER, RUSSELL. "Little Rock Nine Awarded Medal." *The New York Times*, 12 July 1958, www.timesmachine.nytimes.com/timesmachine/1958/07 /12/91395470.html.

RONAN, THOMAS P. "Malcolm X Tells Rally in Harlem Kennedy Fails to Help Negroes." *The New York Times*, 30 June 1963, www.timesmachine.nytimes .com/timesmachine/1963/06/30/356928312.html.

RUGABER, WALTER. "Plea by Mrs. King: 'Fulfill His Dream'." *The New York Times*, 7 Apr. 1968, www.timesmachine.nytimes.com/timesmachine/1968 /04/07/170440732.html.

SAMUELS, GERTRUDE. "Little Rock: More Tension Than Ever." *The New York Times*, 23 Mar. 1958, www.timesmachine.nytimes.com/timesmachine/1958 /03/23/89068370.html.

SAMUELS, GERTRUDE. "Student From Little Rock." *The New York Times*, 24 May 1959, www.timesmachine.nytimes.com/timesmachine/1959 /05/24/437062792.html.

SCHUMACH, MURRAY. "Martin Luther King Jr.: Leader of Millions in Nonviolent Drive for Racial Justice." *The New York Times*, 5 Apr. 1968, www .timesmachine.nytimes.com/timesmachine/1968/04/05/90666312.html.

SITTON, CLAUDE. "5 Negroes Beaten by Mississippi Mob." *The New York Times*, 30 Nov. 1961, www.timesmachine.nytimes.com/timesmachine /1961/11/30/101488040.html.

SITTON, CLAUDE. "Group Maps Plans on Freedom Rides." *The New York Times*, 1 June 1961, www.timesmachine.nytimes.com/timesmachine /1961/06/01/97603318.html.

SITTON, CLAUDE. "How Jim Crow Travels in South." *The New York Times*, 4 June 1961, www.timesmachine.nytimes.com/timesmachine/1961/06 /04/118912973.html.

SITTON, CLAUDE. "Montgomery Tension High After Threats of Bombing." *The New York Times*, 23 May 1961, www.timesmachine.nytimes.com /timesmachine/1961/05/23/97239456.html.

SITTON, CLAUDE. "Negroes to Rally Today in Georgia." *The New York Times*,

21 July 1962, www.timesmachine.nytimes.com/timesmachine/1962/07 /21/102748238.html.

SITTON, CLAUDE. "27 Bi-Racial Bus Riders Are Jailed in Jackson, Miss., as They Extend Campaign." *The New York Times*, 25 May 1961, www .timesmachine.nytimes.com/timesmachine/1961/05/25/97239968.html.

TEAGUE, ROBERT L. "Negroes Say Conditions in U.S. Explain Nationalists' Militancy." *The New York Times*, 2 Mar. 1961, www.timesmachine.nytimes .com/timesmachine/1961/03/02/118025051.html.

WICKER, TOM. "President Supports Travel Right of All." *The New York Times*, 20 July 1961, www.timesmachine.nytimes.com/timesmachine/1961/07/20 /98442134.html.

WILKERSON, ISABEL. "Young Believe Malcolm X Is Still Speaking to Them." *The New York Times*, 18 Nov. 1992, www.nytimes.com/1992/11/18/us /young-believe-malcolm-x-is-still-speaking-to-them.html.

Index

This book is current up until the time of printing. For the most up-to-date reporting, visit www.nytimes.com.